HARRYMOON

HARRY'S CHRISTMAS CAROL

by
Mark Andrew Poe

Illustrations by Becky Minor
Based on the artwork of Christina Weidman

rabbit publishers

Harry's Christmas Carol (Harry Moon)
by Mark Andrew Poe
© Copyright 2017 by Mark Andrew Poe. All rights reserved.

Rabbit Publishers
1624 W. Northwest Highway
Arlington Heights, IL 60004

Illustrations by Christina Weidman
Cover design by Megan Black
Interior design by Lewis Design & Marketing
Creative Consultants: David Kirkpatrick, Thom Black, and Paul Lewis

ISBN: 978-1-943785-67-4

10 9 8 7 6 5 4 3 2 1

1. Fiction - Action and Adventure 2. Children's Fiction
First Color Edition
Printed in U.S.A.

I am your amazing compass, Harry Moon. I can point you to the North Star. But you, not me, are the one who must fly to it.

~ *Rabbit*

Table of Contents

PROLOGUE

Halloween visited the little town of Sleepy Hollow and never left.

Many moons ago, a sly and evil mayor found the powers of darkness helpful in building Sleepy Hollow into "Spooky Town," one of the country's most celebrated attractions. Now, years later, a young eighth-grade magician, Harry Moon, is chosen by the powers of light to do battle against the mayor and his evil consorts.

Welcome to the world of of Harry Moon. Darkness may have found a home in Sleepy Hollow, but if young Harry has anything to say about it, darkness will not be staying.

FAMILY, FRIENDS & FOES

Harry Moon

Harry is the thirteen-year-old hero of Sleepy Hollow. He is a gifted magician who is learning to use his abilities and understand what it means to possess the real magic.

An unlikely hero, Harry is shorter than his classmates and has a shock of inky, black hair. He loves his family and his town. Along with his friend Rabbit, Harry is determined to bring Sleepy Hollow back to its true and wholesome glory.

Rabbit

Now you see him. Now you don't. Rabbit is Harry Moon's friend. Some see him. Most can't.

Rabbit is a large, black-and-white, lop-eared Harlequin rabbit. As Harry has discovered, having a friend like Rabbit has its consequences. Never stingy with advice and counsel, Rabbit always has Harry's back as Harry battles the evil that has overtaken Sleepy Hollow.

Honey Moon

She's a ten-year-old, sassy spitfire. And she's Harry's little sister. Honey likes to say she goes where she is needed, and sometimes this takes her into the path of danger.

Honey never gives in and never gives up when it comes to righting a wrong. Honey always looks out for her friends. Honey does not like that her town has been plunged into a state of eternal Halloween and is even afraid of the evil she feels lurking all around. But if Honey has anything to say about it, evil will not be sticking around.

Samson Dupree

Samson is the enigmatic owner of the Sleepy Hollow Magic Shoppe. He is Harry's mentor and friend. When needed, Samson teaches Harry new tricks and helps him understand his gift of magic.

Samson arranged for Rabbit to become Harry's sidekick and friend. Samson is a timeless, eccentric man who wears purple robes, red slippers, and a gold crown. Sometimes, Samson shows up in mysterious ways. He even appeared to Harry's mother shortly after Harry's birth.

III

Mary Moon

Strong, fair, and spiritual, Mary Moon is Harry and Honey's mother. She is also mother to two-year-old Harvest. Mary is married to John Moon.

Mary is learning to understand Harry and his destiny. So far, she is doing a good job letting Harry and Honey fight life's battles. She's grateful that Rabbit has come alongside to support and counsel her. But like all moms, Mary often finds it difficult to let her children walk their own paths. Mary is a nurse at Sleepy Hollow Hospital.

John Moon

John is the dad. He's a bit of a nerd. He works as an IT professional, and sometimes, he thinks he would love it if his children followed in his footsteps. But he respects that Harry, Honey, and possibly Harvest will need to go their own way. John owns a classic sports car he calls Emma.

Titus Kligore

Titus is the mayor's son. He is a bully of the first degree but also quite conflicted when it comes to Harry. The two have managed to forge a tentative friendship, although Titus will assert his bully strength on Harry from time to time.

Titus is big. He towers over Harry. But in a kind of David vs. Goliath way, Harry has learned which tools are best to counteract Titus's assaults while most of the Sleepy Hollow kids fear him. Titus would probably rather not be a bully, but with a dad like Maximus Kligore, he feels trapped in the role.

Maximus Kligore

The epitome of evil, nastiness, and greed, Maximus Kligore is the mayor of Sleepy Hollow. To bring in the cash, Maximus turned the town into the nightmarish Halloween attraction it is today.

He commissions the evil-tinged celebrations in town. Maximus is planning to take Sleepy Hollow with him to Hell. But will he? He knows Harry Moon is a threat to his dastardly ways, and try as he might, he has yet to rid Harry from his evil plans.

Kligore lives on Folly Farm and owns most of the town, including the town newspaper.

PRELUDE

Harry stood on the rooftop of Declan Dickinson's house. The roof was steepled, and the helidrone Declan got for Christmas was stuck, lodged firmly on the peak. Harry was the designated climber. It wasn't quite Mount Everest, but the bright Christmas icicle lights edging the rooftop reflected an important summit.

"Careful there, bro!" Declan yelled.

"I am," replied Harry in almost a whisper.

"These boots can grip on ice!"

"Not you, bro, be careful with my heli!" cried Declan. Easy for Declan to say. He stood on the snowy ground looking up with Hao and Bailey, members of the Good Mischief Team.

Harry wiggled out the helidrone lodged in the shingles. He brushed the snow and ice from it. That helidrone was sweet. Cyan-blue body. Silver rotors. Built-in camera. Brand new. Technically, it wasn't really Declan's yet, for it wasn't quite Christmas. Declan was "previewing" it from its tidy wrappings in the attic while his parents were out shopping. He had to get it back and rewrapped in one piece.

"Bring it over to the gutter, Moon, so we can see!" shouted Bailey who was viewing the helidrone's camera through his iPhone. Inching his feet along carefully, Harry side-stepped down the high slope of the icy roof. As Harry approached the edge, Bailey shouted, "Drop it, Harry!"

Harry held the drone away from his body

and released the drone from his fingers. Its rotors coming to life, and lights blinking, it shot upward like a rocket ship.

"Whoop! Whoop! Go, baby, go!" shouted Hao. As it soared into the dark winter sky, all eyes and iPhones were on it.

No one noticed Harry's expression grow white as Samson Dupree's sending arrow penetrated his skin, his bone, his mind.

3

His eyes fell into the sparkle where life overcomes death.

He slipped down from the gutter. His body hung suspended in winter air.

"I'll see you tomorrow, guys!" Harry shouted. "Have to go."

The boys looked up. Harry was gone.

4

Verse One

CHRISTMASTIME

On the twelfth day of Christmas,
My drive-through gave to me:
Twelve bags of Pepto,
Eleven pounds of blubber,

Ten baked potatoes,
Nine Polish hot dogs,
Eight bowls of chili,
Seven pints of cole slaw,
Six vanilla milkshakes,
Five on-i-on rings!
Four taco shells,
Three french fries,
Two chocolate bars,
and a big bacon classic with cheese!

This carol was appropriate for the time, but it was in a very different rhyme. The song played across Sleepy Hollow's town green from speakers anchored in the trees. The busy shoppers kept time to its cadence.

Looking out on the rooftop from the Witching Hour Candy Shop on the far east side of Conical Hat Avenue, Sleepy Hollow appeared, to the casual observer, like any other small New England town at Christmastime.

It was storybook bright with what was obviously typical holiday cheer.

Green garlands hung from the storefronts.

Red-and-white candy cane stripes ran down the light posts.

But not so fast. That was looking at the Sleepy Hollow village square from a distance.

If you happened to move in a little closer, stepping out at street level from Dracu-Latte, the bakery and coffee shop on Main Street, you would find your view a bit puzzling.

Green dragon tails formed the garlands on the storefronts.

Fake blood twisted into white bandages created the candy cane illusions on the light posts.

This was a Christmas storybook gone really wrong.

"Bah! Humbug!" a shopper blathered, rushing across Magic Row, his breath floating upward in the cold air.

"Bah! Humbug!" a customer replied. They both laughed, their literary interplay making them both cheerful.

A passerby window shopping through Sleepy Hollow at Christmas would take in a sizeable eyeful that was stranger still.

Through the window at the Screaming Jelly Bean, you would certainly observe the huge glass bowls of blue jellybeans labeled Penguin Poop or the purple jellybeans of Reindeer Poop. The purple jellybeans always sold out early. By the time mid-December rolled around, which is the time of this story, red-and-green-swirled jellybeans called Elf Poop had already replaced them.

Browsing the Christmas window of Chillie Willies Costume Shop, you could watch an elaborate display of an animatronic Bad Santa scolding a sweet little grandma and grandpa all snuggled up in their beds. With visions of sugar-plums dancing in their heads, they happened to forget to leave Bad Santa his Christmas cookies and milk, and he was none too happy.

CHRISTMASTIME

Yes, if you looked closer, it would be clear.

Sleepy Hollow was like no other place on earth.

It was beginning to look a lot like Christmas in Sleepy Hollow, Massachusetts.

But it wasn't the look of the place. It wasn't the smell and feel of the Hollow's square. There was no fragrance of peppermint or balsam. Absent was the aroma of steaming cocoa swirling inside a hot porcelain cup. There was only the loud audio system, spewing out parodies of the Christmas classics through the speakers mounted in the trees.

Jingle bells, Santa smells,
A hundred miles away,
He blows his nose into Cheerios,
And eats 'em every day. Hey!

Of course, everyone likes a little fun at Christmastime. That's part of the tradition. Getting together with friends and family was a royal blast. Jokes and gags. Maybe a few scares are even appropriate over the holidays. After all, wasn't Charles Dicken's *A Christmas Carol* a ghost story about Christmas?

Who didn't get a little queasy in the dark of Christmas morning when there were sounds that might be coming from the wintry visitor from the sky? What's that sound in the chimney? What were those bumps in the night echoing through the house? Was that really Old Saint Nick?

Might we expect some monsters, some creeps, some passing-through-walls, from this Christmas tale in such a ghoulish habitat? Especially when we are writing of our good friend, Harry Moon, at Christmastime? For Harry Moon is a hero, and as it is said of angels— where angels tread, trouble is sure to follow— such can also be said of Harry Moon. Darkness did not make it easy for Harry Moon. And Harry did not help matters with his taunts.

"Bring it on," Harry said.

That certainly did not help.

10

But the dreaded focus of Halloween had not become the theme for Christmas with the Moon family, at least, not yet. In their two-story, modest home on Nightingale Lane, the entire Moon family was getting ready for the merry in Christmas. Unlike the parody Christmas music that played on the green, it remained the classic Christmas carols at the Moon household.

It came upon the midnight clear,
That glorious song of old,
From angels bending near the earth
To touch their harps of gold:
"Peace on the earth, goodwill to men,"
From heaven's all-gracious King.
The world in solemn stillness lay,
To hear the angels sing.

11

Mary and Honey Moon made snowflake cookies in the kitchen. Harry and Harvest Moon along with the hound, Half Moon, set up the train set in the great room of the house. All they needed to complete the holiday was the Christmas tree, which Harry and John Moon would pick up on Saturday from the

Treeodin Tree Fair. This year, it was Harry's turn to pick out the tree, an enormous assignment for any eighth grader. He was already dreaming of that perfect tree for the Moon great room.

The man behind the Halloweeny vision of Sleepy Hollow, Mayor Maximus Kligore, did not have a heart for Christmas. No, not even a little bit. For Maximus Kligore, it was all about making money every day of the year. And it was all about Halloween at Christmastime for Kligore. Of course, there is nothing wrong with making money. Money puts food on tables, gas in the tank, and books in our book bags. But, as the Great Magician said, people cannot live on bread alone.

Truth be told, in Sleepy Hollow, for the last fifteen years, the Spirit of Christmas had been pushed aside for the sake of the almighty buck. Tourists came from as far as Beijing to see the town where every day was Halloween night. "Disneyland means magic. Hollywood means movies. Sleepy Hollow is Halloween," Mayor Maximus Kligore would say at the Sleepy Hollow town meeting. "There is too much marketing and advertising clutter out there, my friends! Sleepy Hollow is not about anything else. It is not about Easter or Christmas or the Fourth of July. A vacation destination has to be about one thing and one thing only. Give the customers what they want. Sleepy Hollow is about *Halloween!*"

A forceful voice in a time of fear has great power. And while the good people of Sleepy Hollow knew better, they were frightened of their worst nightmare—not having enough money for food and gas and books for their book bags. Despite their better selves, they stepped in line with the mayor's vision. They were ready to turn Sleepy Hollow into a town that supported Halloweeny tourism at the cost of almost everything else in their lives. With the construction of the mythic Headless Horseman statue in the center of town fifteen years earlier, the spirit of the common good vanished for good, and the frightened people began the transformation of Sleepy Hollow into "Spooky Town."

13

Kligore knew what he was doing. From around the world, people came to climb up on the gigantic saddle of the Headless Horseman statue and get their picture snapped to share with family and friends on Instagram and Snapchat and Facebook. The people traveled from near and far to be amused by the witches, unsparkly vampires, and warlocks that roamed the streets, all characters from the costumed Sleepy Hollow Fright Squad. The Fright Squad was like the Mickey and Minnie characters at Disneyland, but they were not funny or sweet in the least. The Fright Squad characters were disgustingly awful.

The people bought their Sleepy Hollow souvenirs of cauldrons, Headless Horseman dolls, and glittering wands, largely products manufactured by one of Mayor Kligore's many companies. They shopped at I.C. Dead People and ate lunch at the Haunted Wood Brasserie. You bet they came, from all over. The town delivered Halloween night on every day of the year. And Halloween conquered big time.

Not that there was anything wrong with Halloween. But to live inside it, 24/7, that was quite another matter.

CHRISTMASTIME

To survive, the good people of Sleepy Hollow took the long, slippery slope down to the lowest edge of themselves.

Initially, it was Kligore's commercial decision to turn the town sideways. As the years moved on, the Hollow's people became less like real people. There was less jogging in the park. Less laughter at the movies. Less charity in the Christmas season.

It was the adults that suffered this disintegration more than the kids.

After all, kids were kids. They were still learning and growing and reaching out to touch the sky. They had friends and sports and dances and sleepovers and their own growing pains to occupy their time.

Back at the beginning of the town's makeover where streets went from Wheeler and Adams to Magic Row and Witch Broom, a strange man from a distant land moved into town.

He was a most peculiar little fellow with

twinkling eyes and a mischievous smile.

He wore a plastic crown of gold, a purple cape sprinkled with silver stars, and shiny red shoes. He was a smidgen stout, not much to look at, and entirely forgettable except for his weirdo props and those sparkling eyes. No one in Sleepy Hollow thought much about him. No one ever had. His little shop, the Sleepy Hollow Magic Shoppe, seemed to fit right in, curiously enough, with the one thing the town was selling. Halloween. But the Sleepy Hollow Magic Shoppe never seemed to do much business except for the business of one boy. Harry Moon, now thirteen and in eighth grade at Sleepy Hollow Middle School, was its regular visitor. He seemed to be its most consistent and faithful customer. Except, of course, at Christmastime.

Randy Toledo, owner of the Toledo Barbershop, appeared to be the peculiar fellow's only friend. But even Randy could not put his finger on the strange gentleman's lineage. He was not German or Chinese or Italian. What was he?

He had a French surname, Dupree.

His first name was Samson, like the mythic figure who held his strength in his hair. But, that was just the thing. About Samson Dupree's hair. And it would be the barber, Randy Toledo, who knew this best. Samson's jet-black hair never seemed to grow.

Like the great Clock Tower in the town green that struck a bell every hour on the hour, Samson Dupree appeared at the barbershop on time every week to get his hair cut. With a friendly nod, he climbed into the chair. Randy went to work.

"Just a trim today, Randy."

Randy Toledo snip-snip-snipped with his scissors. He snipped about the ears. He lopped around the neck. But there was nothing to trim.

Samson Dupree had plenty of hair. Samson was old, but his hair had no gray. It was jet black and sat like a plate of burnt pancakes atop his head. It was sometimes hard to tell what was up there because of the crown he often wore.

Randy lathered up Samson's neck with hot foam and gave the peculiar little man a close shave with a sharp straight razor. But there was nothing to shave.

Meanwhile, Samson swapped stories and told jokes with the customers. They caught each other up on the latest news. Samson became the life of the barbershop. Once in a while, Samson would even amuse the shop with a magic trick. His crown exploded in red fire. He pulled a rabbit out of his shoe with his foot still in the shoe.

Were these tricks or were they magic?

Randy Toledo never asked Samson Dupree about why his hair never grew. Instead, there was this exchange, told in a kind of code of small-town civility.

"I hate to charge you, my man," Randy Toledo said.

"Oh, think nothing of it," Samson Dupree replied with a laugh. "You are a most excellent barber, Randy Toledo!"

One night, Randy saw Samson standing on Magic Row, looking at the square. There, the costumed ghosts and warlocks in the Fright Squad were running about the town, scaring the heck out of tourists wanting to be

19

scared. Blood-curdling screams and ghostly *bwahaaaas* would emanate from the speakers throughout the square. Meanwhile, Samson just watched. The magician breathed in the fresh air of the small country town. He grinned as if all the world were beautiful.

"What are you smiling at, my man?" Randy asked Samson.

"I am smiling at all the people," Samson replied. Randy looked into Samson's face against the dark night. Samson's eyes twinkled like a star field. "I just love people. Can't get enough of them."

That night, Randy Toledo figured it out. Samson Dupree did not come to the barbershop for a shave, for he never really needed one. He came for the conversation. He came for the fun of the people. Samson loved people.

Which might have been the strangest thing of all, Randy thought, because Samson felt oddly not human at all.

But that night, Randy Toledo finally understood why Samson Dupree had come into their small, evil town.

He had come to save Sleepy Hollow from itself.

It was three days before Christmas. The brilliant, but diabolically greedy, Mayor Maximus Kligore stomped into Randy Toledo's barbershop. He noticed the holiday decoration at the entrance.

"That Christmas wreath on your door, Mr. Toledo, there is no Halloween in the garlands," said the mayor. "Lose it now."

"With respect, Mayor, I am not required to sheath my wreath in serpent heads and dragon tails like every other store on this street. I can do what I choose. I choose Christmas."

"Perhaps you should review the bylaws for

storefront properties, you sad barber." The mayor's voice tightened and eyes narrowed as he heard the song on the radio inside of the barbershop play.

Joy to the World, the Lord is come!
Let earth receive her King;
Let every heart prepare Him room,
And Heaven and nature sing,
And Heaven and nature sing,
And Heaven, and Heaven, and nature sing.

Kligore hung his overcoat on the wall hook and walked over to the shelf where the antique wooden radio played. He turned the knob quickly until it settled on the mayor's We Drive By Night radio station, the Sleepy Hollow Outburst. He smiled in a twisted yuletide grin as the music played.

Rudolf, the red-nosed reindeer,
Had a very bloody nose,
And if you ever saw him,
You would really think he blows!

And so our Christmas tale begins in Sleepy

CHRISTMASTIME

Hollow. As most tales do in Sleepy Hollow, our tale begins in blood. Look closely, for this tiny trickle of crimson liquid will set off a firestorm of malevolence that only Harry Moon might be able to douse.

24

Verse Two

SOMETHING WICKED THIS WAY COMES

Randy Toledo was hopping mad. The mayor was even controlling the radio waves in his small barbershop.

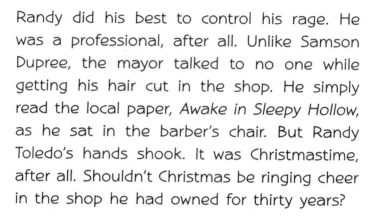

Randy did his best to control his rage. He was a professional, after all. Unlike Samson Dupree, the mayor talked to no one while getting his hair cut in the shop. He simply read the local paper, *Awake in Sleepy Hollow*, as he sat in the barber's chair. But Randy Toledo's hands shook. It was Christmastime, after all. Shouldn't Christmas be ringing cheer in the shop he had owned for thirty years?

As he was shaving Mayor Kligore's neck, Randy Toledo slipped with the straight razor. It sliced through the hot foam and nicked Kligore's skin. It was a small cut, like a paper slice. But you would have thought it was murder the way the mayor grabbed his neck and screamed. He yelled the Very Bad Words at the barber. Kligore called Randy Toledo an incompetent and the worst barber in the world, among many other things. He threatened to shut the barbershop down and throw Randy Toledo in jail.

Even though it was a small cut, the blood splattered over the collar of Kligore's white shirt as he screamed, making it appear much worse than it was.

Randy felt as defeated as any human being could ever feel. As the mayor berated him, Randy felt as low as the townspeople. Everyone in the town was forgetting who they were. They escaped to a safe life in their servitude to Spooky Town and a retreat from Kligore's wrath. The mayor got inside everyone's head, and now he was inside Randy Toledo's.

With a loud BAM, the shop door crashed open to the tirade of the Very Bad Words. The peculiar little man with the plastic crown from the magic shop next door appeared. He stepped before the barber's chair where Kligore was carrying on, screaming at Randy Toledo.

27

"Get out of here, Maximus, this instant. You are not wanted in this establishment. Randy Toledo is a most excellent barber!"

"I am so sorry, Mr. Mayor," whispered Randy, his face flushed in red embarrassment as he handed the mayor a Band-Aid.

"See?" shouted Samson Dupree, his plastic,

gold crown atop his head. "He is sorry."

Mayor Maximus Kligore pulled his blood-stained towel from around his neck, threw it on the floor, and raised himself up to his full, very tall height. His face was taut with hate and anger. His lips opened over his teeth. His jaw was clenched in a grimace of disdain.

"He cut me on purpose, Dupree!" cried the mayor.

"It was an honest mistake," said Samson.

"I am really terribly sorry, Mayor," Randy Toledo said, again and again.

"Stand down, Mayor Maximus Kligore," said Samson Dupree. "Or you will not be standing at all!"

Mayor Maximus Kligore was six foot two. He was much taller than Samson. From this view, the mayor could take Samson down in a heartbeat. But in looking closer still, Randy Toledo watched the mayor step back as if there was a force field in front of him. Randy sensed they knew each other from some ancient war, from the tales of old.

Without another word, a mumbling Maximus snatched his overcoat from the hook on the wall. He yanked the door open in a huff, pulled the little green wreath from its place, and threw it on the ground before stomping on it on his way out of the barbershop.

29

Through the window, Randy Toledo and Samson Dupree watched Maximus Kligore stamp down Main Street. "Samson?" asked Randy. "How did you know I was in trouble?"

"I have history with Kligore at this time of year," Samson said.

Fire flashed in the peculiar magician's eyes. Randy knew enough about spirit to understand this was not the fire of punishment. This was the fire of a sanctified imagination.

"I have been facing down men like

Maximus for centuries," Samson said. "It is not right for him to bully you, Randy. You are a kind man and a most excellent barber."

It was then that Randy Toledo understood. This was not about a nick to the neck. This was not about a wreath without dragon's tails. This was not about Halloweeny storefront rules.

Sleepy Hollow was built on sacred ground. There was a vortex of highly-desired energy off of Mayflower Road.

Their small town was the latest battlefield in an ancient war, the war between good and evil.

And Sleepy Hollow was the prize.

From the door, Randy Toledo watched the strange little man in his cloak and red shoes tip his gold crown as he bid farewell. As he did, Samson picked up the mangled balsam wreath. He straightened the red bow and placed it back on the door.

"Thank you, Samson," Randy Toledo said.

"You are my friend," replied Samson. "Think nothing of it."

That afternoon, sunset came early. The wind was bitter with chill. Braving the cold snap in the air, Samson Dupree pulled the red-and-green Christmas scarf that Harry Moon's mom, Mary Moon, had knitted for him over his chin and mouth. Snowflakes whirled as the brick Clock Tower in the green struck seven bells. Samson trundled across the snow-dusted center of town.

31

A ridiculous parody of "God Rest Ye Merry Gentlemen" blasted over the audio system. But, there was another song playing in the far distance. If you listened very closely to the wind, you just might hear its evil cadence. It was the dirge of devilry coming from the speakers at Folly Farm.

By the pricking of my thumbs,
Something wicked this way comes!
Doors, unlock,
To whoever knocks!

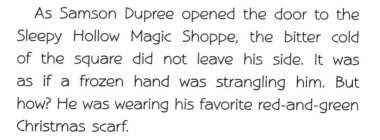

As Samson Dupree opened the door to the Sleepy Hollow Magic Shoppe, the bitter cold of the square did not leave his side. It was as if a frozen hand was strangling him. But how? He was wearing his favorite red-and-green Christmas scarf.

He looked around the shop that held so much charm and which he loved so much. There were the magic top hats, white rabbits, and wands on a high shelf. A grand, silver castle made from Modbot construction bricks stood in the center of the shop. It was so beautiful, like a castle from a fairy tale.

A full net of Magic 8 Balls, a popular seller at Christmas, hung from the ceiling. There were the characters in the corner shelf—Gepetto, the toymaker from Pinocchio, Red Riding Hood, and the Archangel, Michael, in bright gold wings, brandishing a silver sword. Action figures of the world's most famous wizards—Merlin, Elvis Gold, Gandalf, and Dumbledore—stood upon another corner display.

One day, Samson thought, an action figure of Harry Moon might just join the starry lineup.

The Sleepy Hollow lad, Harry Moon, was precisely the reason why Samson Dupree had climbed out of time and arrived in the small town fourteen years ago. Samson had arrived before Harry was born. He came to lay the way for the boy.

Samson was the great teacher to Merlin, to the archangel Michael, and to Harry's great-great-grandfather, Astronomer Moon. But Astronomer, a brilliant mathematician, had been tragically killed in London, England by a deadly spell. This time, Samson Dupree needed to get it right with Harry Moon. But in the meanwhile, the devilish dirge of Folly Farm was taking hold of the air inside the magic shop. Samson was so overcome with cold, he neither heard the diabolical music nor did he notice the cloud of spiders moving over the silver Modbot castle.

33

Hundreds of black spiders fell across the castle ramparts like heavy doomed snowflakes. They crawled through the castle and out the drawbridge. They scattered across the floor. They climbed the walls of the magic shop.

Under the curse of Kligore's song, Samson Dupree fell into a deep sleep on a wooden chair. The silver glasses of Gepetto glinted from the shelf. It was the shadow falling on Pinocchio's legendary maker. Spiders crawled

out of Gepetto's kindly mouth and scattered furiously throughout the store as if it was the opening of their breeding cave. It was a disgusting and horrifying scene for a quite cheery magic shop.

With the hemlock dug-up in the dark,
And the ravenous bone of the salt-sea
*   shark!*
By the pricking of my thumbs,
Something wicked this way comes!

36

Verse Three

CALL ME B. L. ZEBUB

Silvered in the moon's eclipse,
In Samson's Dupree's nose and lips,
Once the shadow works as could,
Then the charm is firm and good!

The incendiary incantation rang out from the bowels of Folly Farm. Snow swirled. From every window of Mayor Kligore's evil home, an electric candlestick shone in celebration of the Halloweeny holiday. At a distance, the sweeping estate of the candlelit manse, stables, and outbuildings looked like a picturesque Christmas card.

But what were those gleaming candlesticks welcoming from the windowpanes? It was not the joyful spirit of the season. For over the front door hung a somber black wreath, woven from the dreaded *Atropa belladonna* plant, commonly known as deadly nightshade. One bite from the berry of the nightshade stopped a human heart in three minutes. This doomed wreath welcomed the spirit of destruction during the most joyous season of the year.

Three floors beneath the estate was the Kligore bunker, built in the 1920s. It was forged by the Masterlock Company that developed the strongest of materials to protect the military's most sensitive and advanced equipment. Now, the vault was the property of Kligore's We Drive

By Night Company and guarded by the dark side's most impenetrable forces.

The board of the We Drive by Night Company convened in the dark room known as the Grotto because it possessed a cavernous-like essence. Carved into the stone over the largest cave were some of evil's most terrible resources —jealousy, hatred, and discord. There was a great stone hearth with a massive, roaring fire. The ceilings dripped with stalactites. Bats nestled in the dark recesses. Snakes slithered in the green puddles within the caverns.

This is all to say that, at the Grotto, the board members felt favorably at home. Everyone stood at the star table and sang somberly to the black, three-legged pot steaming in the center of the table. Maximus Kligore, the CEO of We Drive By Night, stood at the head of the table. The blood from the barbershop incident still rimmed his collar. He closed his eyes and listened to the Fouling Curse. It was the most powerful spell known anywhere. It needed to be if it was going help him to take down Samson Dupree once and for all.

39

40

The Imperial Captain of Dragons, Lady Dra Dra, her puke-lemon wig swinging, led the voices of destruction in the creepy carol.

Like a charm of powerful trouble,
Like a hell-broth boil and bubble,
Double, double toil and trouble,
Fire burn and cauldron bubble!

The disgusting hound of hell, Oink, sang from a pointed ray of the star. Next to him was his diligent assistant, Ug, a rodent-like critter with silver eyes and an awful, off-key voice. A group of robed figures sang next to Ug. Their faces could not be seen beneath the shadow of their cowls, if they had faces at all. The flashily dressed admins for the company, Cherry Tomato and Booboo Hoodoo, were boisterous.

Silvered in the moon's eclipse,
In Samson Dupree's nose and lips,
Once the shadow works as could,
Then the charm is firm and good!

41

With the finale of the incantation, a gush came from the magical concoction. Spurting from the mouth of the three-legged pot was a whorl of corrupting spirits. Brandishing their demolishing swords, they swam into the trickling stalactites and disappeared into the grounds above.

Maximus Kligore applauded the spirited arousal.

"I must commend you, Lady Dra Dra," cheered Maximus, "that new little ditty appears to be quite effective."

"I started it as soon as I got your call from outside the barber shop. I despise that twerp, Samson Dupree. It's time we finish him off! But *little ditty*, Dark Lord?" Lady Dra Dra said with a huff. "That is from William Shakespeare! And it's hardly new. It's four hundred years old!"

"Shakespeare?" Maximus Kligore asked. "According to the *Secret Histories*, we were close, but we never got the old guy over to our side."

"That doesn't mean we can't use his lovely words for evil! It's rule *numero uno*! We use all that is good, turning it, if at all possible, toward discouragement. And discouragement most often leads to our favorite word."

"Destruction," called the demons of the board.

"I can't hear you!" Lady Dra Dra shouted back. She twisted her gray tail and turned it into a hearing horn next to her pointed ear.

"DESTRUCTION!" the demons screamed.

"Ahhh, much better!" she said.

As the hardy hail of shouting continued, Lady Dra Dra became exhilarated. Smiling as her team shouted her favorite word, she slithered across the floor. She looked at the blood on her CEO's collar and shook her head of vomit-yellow hair with a "Tsk, tsk, tsk" at Maximus.

She brought her taloned hands to his neck and magically brushed her fingers across his shirt collar. With a hiss, the dried blood vaporized. The shirt was new again.

43

"There you go, Boss Man," she said. "You want to look good for our chairman."

"Our chairman? What do you mean?" Maximus said with a nervous tinge.

"Hadn't you heard? Mr. B. L. Zebub is coming to see you."

There was a choking sound from the floor below. The fire in the hearth leaped into flames. Red-hot energy licked the sides of the hearth.

"See me?" cried Maximus.

"As a matter of fact, he has just arrived," replied Lady Dra Dra, bowing to the flames as they roared. The elevator doors opened to the molten center of the world and the private lair of B.L. Zebub himself.

Stepping through the hearth was a most magnificent creature. This was a shape-shifter of enormous ability. When the Great Magician had seen B.L. Zebub in the desert, he shouted, "Get behind me, Satan!" And Zebub did, for the power of the Great Magician exceeded his.

Indeed, Zebub was the false god that men or women or boys or girls could just not seem to get behind them. B.L. Zebub ruled them—with their want for power, fame, fortune, or just that special Bluetooth device that someone might crave too rabidly for Christmas.

B. L. Zebub could also come in the form of alcohol or drugs or food. He was a sinister beast.

Depending on the uniqueness of the person, B. L. Zebub would shape-shift into anyone or anything that became the great struggle of any one life. He might appear in the desire for the beautiful cheerleader or the handsome quarterback or the high-flying drone or the gorgeous party dress. B. L. Zebub filled the bill for any unbridled craving and would wreck the souls and hearts and minds of people through their uncontrollable yearnings.

45

From a distance, B. L. Zebub was a whirl of storm and color and wind. But step closer. While in the particular shoes of Maximus Kligore, his drug of choice was a city of blinding gold before him. Through Oink's eyes, the hound of hell slobbered at an all-you-can-eat sirloin steak takeout open 24/7. Zebub was oh-so-good at what he did.

Nervously, in his fresh white shirt, Maximus Kligore dropped to a knee before the city of blinding gold, also known as Mr. B. L. Zebub.

"Who told you to move today on the destruction of Samson Dupree?" shouted B. L. Zebub.

"It was time, Master." The usually formidable Maximus Kligore whimpered like a child.

"It is not time, you imbecile! We move when human beings aren't thinking! We catch them off guard at the beach or at the theater during a bad movie. Not in prime time. Not at Christmas when everyone is dreaming and feeling all those lofty thoughts of goodness and ridiculous frivolity!"

Maximus Kligore pulled himself together in defense. He got off his knees and brushed the smudges off his pants. "We have shut down twelve of the thirteen churches in this town and both synagogues!" said Kligore to the "city of gold." He smoothed the wrinkles from his knees with the flat of his hands. "We have got the people in this town so full of fear that they can't think about anything but staying in the grind and making money! Once I get Samson Dupree, that stinking herald of light, out of the picture, Harry Moon will go down. Without that protection, the sacred vortex will be ours!"

"Or is it that your own passions are getting the better of you, Kligore? Do you just happen to want to bring Samson down on *this* day of all days out of spite because he defended that barber over your little bloody boo-boo?"

47

Maximus grew red with anger against his boss. "How dare you question the strength of my will? I have sacrificed my family. My wife ran away from me! I have given everything to you, and you treat me now before my company staff like an unpaid intern!"

The swirling, colorful whorls of B.L. Zebub pulled back toward the hearth as if impressed with what his CEO had to say. Then the greatest of the Dark Lords spoke.

"Very well, Kligore, you are the CEO of We Drive By Night, and so I shall abide by your

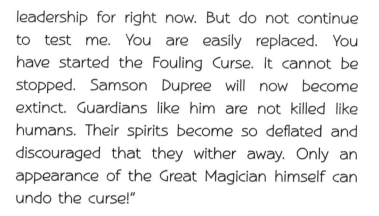

leadership for right now. But do not continue to test me. You are easily replaced. You have started the Fouling Curse. It cannot be stopped. Samson Dupree will now become extinct. Guardians like him are not killed like humans. Their spirits become so deflated and discouraged that they wither away. Only an appearance of the Great Magician himself can undo the curse!"

"What Great Magician?" Lady Dra Dra asked with a laugh. "He has not been around these parts in years!" She laughed merrily.

The Demons of the Board laughed along with the Imperial Captain of Dragons. The colored whorls fell into the punishing flames of the great stone hearth. Then the great evil one known to every soul by a thousand names said its final words as the voice vanished in the flames.

"You, alone, Kligore, and the We Drive By Night Company shall bring us one step further to opening the sacred vortex of Sleepy Hollow," said B. L. Zebub. "Through your efforts, the Great Pains shall be unleashed, and we will end

48

for all time the dream of humankind."

The smoke and flame were one.

50

Verse Four

SAMSON'S ARROW

Evil Mayor Kligore's Fouling Curse had its effect. The celestial body of Samson Dupree lay on the floor of the Sleepy Hollow Magic Shoppe. He had slid limply off the wooden chair in the cold bluster of the bitter spell. An army of spiders, commanded by the action figure Merlin, rolled his golden crown into the corner.

Even though Merlin was nothing more than a possessed action figure, the spiders were not smart enough to know that. Diligently, the hairy, creepy bodies complied with the dark, dull eyes of the plastic wizard.

Samson watched through his sunken eyes as if in a dream. He had no control over the proceedings around him. He did not feel ill, really. No queasy stomach. No headache. It was something far worse. It was the bruising of his inner heart.

The great Samson Dupree, legend of the spiritual realms, had flown through matter. He had traveled through time. But now, he lay in a listless stupor, watching the future of Sleeping Hollow unravel through the eyes of the curse.

His vision was telling him that all his efforts would prove pointless.

The cursed cloud of spiders had stolen his heart.

It was imperative to the eternal story that Samson uphold the hallowed first law of the Heavenly Realms, which was to allow humanity its free will. While he could encourage, guide, and cajole, Samson could never take over. Humans were not lifeless objects. They were not to be pushed and pulled about willy-nilly on a chessboard. That may be the way of We Drive By Night, but it was not Samson's way. Humans needed to make their own choices, to decide for themselves. Indeed, Samson could inspire his young hero, Harry Moon. But it would always be Harry Moon's own decision to grab Samson's inspiration and fight.

In the midst of the magic shop disarray, Merlin's action figure face leered at Samson. For a moment, Samson believed that it was Merlin himself showing his disdain in those dark, dull eyes. Merlin was the wizard Samson had once trained in his boyhood to tutor the once-and-future king of the Round Table.

As he lay on the floor, all Samson could hear was the silly holiday music piping from the speakers in the square:

Wreck the malls this Christmas Season,
Fa la-la-la-la, la-la-la-la;
Blow your cash for no good reason,
Fa la-la-la-la, la-la-la-la;
Push your charge card to the limit,
Fa la-la-la-la, la-la-la-la;
Your checkbook now has nothing in it,
Fa la-la-la-la, la-la-la-la.

Still, in the deepest part of his bruised, bruised heart, Samson remembered Harry Moon's plea. Not too long ago, earlier, in tears, unsure of the magic power growing within, Harry stood before Samson and begged him to never ever leave him.

"I cannot live without you, Samson!" Harry cried. Samson had smiled and patted his young friend on the shoulder lovingly. "I shall remain as long as I am needed, Harry," he had reassured the lad. Now, that was proving not to be true. He was not leaving. He was being taken away before his work was done.

Against the slaughtering moment, Samson's heart pumped with a tiny burst of hope. Harry Moon was not handsome. Harry Moon made many mistakes. But Harry Moon, with his huge heart, tried and tried and tried. He possessed the deep magic. Samson could see the goodness of Harry's smile as if he were standing before him. But it was not Harry standing there to rescue him from the din and mire. It was only the ghostly memory of Harry. And so Samson did what all good Guardians do.

He aimed for the hope of the one he guarded.

Samson Dupree carved a message with his holy mind. He wrapped it in an arrowhead of determination. He shot the arrow from the bow of his supreme will.

Exploding from his celestial corpus, the message flew through the wood in the door of the Sleepy Hollow Magic Shoppe.

It sped above the pavement of Magic Row. It ran past the voices in the town square—

55

Wreck the pet store, do some damage,
Fa la-la-la-la, la-la-la-la;
Send the beagles on a rampage,
Fa la-la-la-la, la-la-la-la;
Acting in an uncouth manner,
Fa la-la-la-la, la-la-la-la;
Drop your drawers and moon that Santa,
Fa la-la-la-la, la-la-la-la.

The supernatural arrow whipped past the steeple of Old North Church. It brushed the maple trees of Nightingale Lane, searching for the hope of the one the Guardian was nurturing—Harry Cornelius Moon.

Harry stood on the rooftop of Declan Dickinson's house. The roof was steepled and the quad-rotor helidrone Declan got for Christmas was stuck, lodged firmly on the peak. Harry was the designated climber. It wasn't quite Mount Everest, but the bright Christmas icicle lights edging the rooftop reflected an important summit.

"Careful there, bro!" Declan yelled.

"I am," replied Harry in almost a whisper. "These boots can grip on ice!"

"Not you, bro, be careful with my heli!" cried Declan. Easy for Declan to say. He stood on the snowy ground looking up with Hao and Bailey, members of the Good Mischief Team.

Harry wiggled out the helidrone lodged in the shingles. He brushed the snow and ice from it. That helidrone was sweet. Cyan-blue body. Silver rotors. Built-in camera. Brand new. Technically, it wasn't really Declan's yet, for it wasn't quite Christmas. Declan was "previewing" it from its tidy wrappings in the attic while his parents were out shopping. He had to get it back and rewrapped in one piece.

"Bring it over to the gutter, Moon, so we can see!" shouted Bailey who was viewing the helidrone's camera through his iPhone. Inching his feet along carefully, Harry side-stepped down the high slope of the icy roof. As Harry approached the edge, Bailey shouted, "Drop it, Harry!"

Harry held the drone out away from his body and released the drone from his fingers. Its rotors coming to life and lights blinking, it shot upward like a rocket ship.

"Whoop! Whoop! Go, baby, go!" shouted Hao. As it soared into the dark winter sky, all eyes and iPhones were on it.

No one noticed Harry's expression grow white as Samson Dupree's sending arrow penetrated his skin, his bone, his mind.

His eyes fell into the sparkle where life overcomes death.

He slipped down from the gutter. His body hung suspended in the winter air.

"I'll see you tomorrow, guys!" Harry shouted. "Have to go."

The boys looked up. Harry was gone.

Declan just shook his head. He knew Harry could take care of himself.

As cool as it was to fly at thirteen, it was becoming harder and harder for Harry Moon to be a regular guy. He wore the best hiking boots that his budget could afford, but did he really need them at all?

Harry had grown a lot in eighth grade, and so had his magic. He was a captive of two worlds—this one and another. Did he need boots? Or did he need wings? Truth is, he needed both.

Months ago, through Samson Dupree's tutelage, Harry had begun flying across Sleepy Hollow when he piloted Impenetrable, Samson's magic carpet.

Now, at this special moment, and by the power of his very own hand, Harry Moon flew through the space that held all life together. For those journeys, Harry needed no magic carpet.

By the power of his own right hand, the hand that wrote notes to his favorite ex-babysitter Sarah Sinclair and the hand that held his cereal spoon, Harry was able to shrink to a size tinier than molecules. Particles flew about like planets as he flew through the tiny spaces between them in what we know in this world as matter. He was pretty fast. His teacher had sent him a prayer. Samson required his help. He would be there in a blink of an eye. Almost.

The Clock Tower gonged with the tenth hour.

In an instant, Harry Moon stood outside the Sleepy Hollow Magic Shoppe. Its cheery yellow-

60

and-white awning above the large display window contrasted with the somber gray and midnight-blue colors of the store's two neighbors—I. C. Dead People and Sleeping Spiders.

Harry took a deep breath and let it out slowly. Something wasn't right. Why didn't he arrive inside the store like he usually did?

He opened his palms and moved his hands over the door like he was feeling for something. The green-and-red wreath, absent of dragon tails, still hung over a small oval window. *Has someone put glamor over the shop?* Harry had never experienced a glamor before. But he knew it was a Hiding Spell. A spell so strong, for blessing or for curse, it made it impossible to penetrate by even the most skillful magician.

61

The door swung open on its own. As powerful as the magic within was becoming, Harry could not discern if the spirits opening the door were evil or good. He entered the shop.

The little doorbell did not chime this time. The familiar tinkle always welcomed Harry to the shop. It was as familiar to Harry as his own name.

It always chimed.

But not this time.

The store was cold and dim. The only light emanated from a strand of tiny Christmas bulbs behind the counter. A rigid Samson, his crown back on his head and in his purple robe, stood behind the cash register. He had an odd look on his face.

"Why, hullo, Harry. What a pleasant surprise," Samson said.

"Samson, what's wrong?" Harry said. He stared into his friend's face. "Are you okay?"

"Why, of course, Harry. Nothing is wrong."

"But I just received a sending from you. It came right to me. Are you in trouble?" Harry

stepped closer to the counter.

"I sent you nothing but my continued good wishes," Samson said. His voice was dry and disengaged.

As he approached, Harry had a most peculiar feeling, almost as peculiar as the clothes Samson Dupree wore. He had the distinct feeling he was being watched. He glanced around the shop. He looked carefully at the great wizards who stood on the shelf— Merlin, Elvis Gold, Gandalf, and Dumbledore.

63

Harry swore the Gepetto figurine turned his head toward him.

"I know it was from Samson. I know the rhythms of my teacher's messages."

"Harry, you are still my student. There is much for you to learn," Samson said. Harry could not see the star field that always twinkled in his teacher's eyes. That always made Harry feel welcomed and cared for. It was hauntingly absent.

"Whoever sent that message to me was my teacher. I know, here and now, you are not my teacher," Harry said. Harry's breath climbed upward in the cold, dark store. He shivered.

"Oh, you tire me, boy," said Samson, turning away to put on his cloak.

"The teacher who cried for help is no longer here," Harry said as he walked behind the register. "What have you done to Samson Dupree?" Anger bubbled inside Harry's stomach. Something was terribly wrong.

"It's late. I'm going to bed."

"Bed?" Harry said. "There is no place for you to put your head. You are not human. Your home is not here!"

The figure of Samson blanched as if Harry had arrived at part of the truth.

Pulling power from his right hand, Harry grabbed the creature, shoving him against the wall.

"I am the mighty Samson! Take your hand off of me!" cried the thing with a prideful roar. As Harry held up his fist to smite the creature, the store popped with sound.

Rat-a-tat-tat! Like steady, powerful machine gun fire.

It was a plundering racket.

The Christmas bulbs exploded on the strand.

Every single light went out, like the candles on a birthday cake.

The store tumbled into utter and complete darkness.

In the wink of an eye, a powerful paw grabbed Harry's shoulders and pulled him through the icy gloom.

66

Verse Five

SHEPHERDS, WHY THIS JUBILEE?

Mayor Kligore's assistant, Lady Dra Dra, now wearing a blood-red wig, stood outside the Sleepy Hollow Magic

Shoppe. She screamed at Harry as he flew through the shop door, just missing her, and out across Magic Row.

"Beat it, punk!" she shouted at the vanishing Harry Moon, her slime-green dragon tail chattering against the sidewalk. "This magic store is ours!"

It was past ten, but the speakers still blasted the twisted tunes of a Sleepy Hollow Christmas.

Jingle bells, jngle bells,
The children tipped the tree;
Priceless ornaments smashed to bits,
The kids each say "not me."

A crowd of tourists, thinking Dra Dra was one of the characters in the Sleepy Hollow Fright Squad, swarmed her, seeking a celebrity answer to their many enthusiastic questions.

"Don't be so surprised. That was all me. I got you out of there," said Rabbit.

Harry flopped down onto a park bench.

Rabbit sat next to him. For such a large bunny, it was interesting that so few people could see him.

"What?" Harry said, his eyes wide. "How did I get here? I was just talking to that Samson look-alike!" Harry's heart pounded, sitting next to his special and wise friend.

"That was me. I sucked you out of the

store before you did something to that Samson creature you would *forever* regret."

"But, Rabbit, that guy is my friend! What happened to Samson, and where is he? He sent me a message. Something tells me he is in trouble. I just want to knock that imposter's head off."

"Precisely my point!" Rabbit said. "You might have taken off his head like a jack-o'-lantern off a scarecrow. Then, where would Samson be? As headless as the statue in the square. Whoever that creature was, he was using Samson's body. Can't take his head off. He'll need it later! Besides, you don't win justice through reckless vengeance, my friend."

"How do I get him back?" Harry stared across Magic Row at the little magic store.

Harry could see through the display window. He saw a dark curtain open. Small, green, worm-like critters crept up from the snowy sidewalk and nestled in the wreath beneath the oval window of the wooden door.

Like tiny watchers, dark-eyed dragons peered at Harry in the circle of the wreath. They taunted him.

"Such a curse as we see in that shop comes from the mouth of hell," Rabbit said. "It is spoken by B. L. Zebub himself. It cannot be defeated by mere physical attack. No, this kind needs a deeper truth." Rabbit rubbed his left ear. "Our dear Samson is presently lost to one of the force's great weapons. Discouragement."

81

"Listen to the way you talk, Rabbit! So casual! Samson doesn't have the flu!" Harry said.

"No, it is definitely not the flu," Rabbit said.

The great harlequin lagomorph crossed his legs. "A terrible and crushing veil has fallen over Samson Dupree's eyes. It extends to the deepest recesses of his soul. Only one thing can raise the shade or surely, very soon, his spirit will be dead to all of us."

"And what is that?" Harry asked.

"Not what." Rabbit said. "Who."

Harry looked across the green. He shuddered at the thought of what was happening to his friend, his mentor, his town.

"The Great Magician," Rabbit said.

"That's impossible."

12

"Harry. This is not some trifling Salem sorceress. This is not even Mayor Kligore. This is the boss of the spiritual underworld." Rabbit stood now on his hind legs. "Zebub does not even believe that the Great Magician still exists. He thinks he was defeated long ago. Of course, he is sadly mistaken."

Harry's heart pounded.

"Show the Dark Lord and his dark army what Christmas is all about. Their eyes have not been drawn to such a sight in quite some time."

"But I am just a kid!" Harry said.

"Have you not put away your childish things? Have you not been receiving Samson's messages to your mind? Are you not flying through matter? Does the Great Magician not watch over you?"

Harry swallowed. He nodded.

"Man up, Harry Moon, for Heaven's sake! You have the toolkit. And that toolkit is your mind, heart, and soul. Look for the signs and wonders. All of life is a big, wide tangle of roads. Me? I am your amazing compass. I can point you to the North Star. But you are the one who must fly to it."

83

Rabbit had a very bouncy nature. He was an expert at arriving and departing from Harry's top hat. From the beginning of his magic shows, Harry won applause from Rabbit's over-the-top theatrics. So Harry knew what was coming. Rabbit's last words were his cue.

Rabbit vanished in a sparkle of icy air, proving

once again that a rabbit can be a ham. But for Harry, the dark and the cold remained.

On the lonely bench, Harry marveled at the dark, supernatural encasement that had fallen over the magic store. His heart ached for what was once his favorite place in Sleepy Hollow.

He knew Samson did not have the flu or any other simple illness. Samson was dying.

74

Harry walked the long way home. The Clock Tower struck the half hour as Harry shuffled down Magic Row toward his home on Nightingale Lane. He loved his mom and dad very much. They helped him out almost always. He loved talking things out. But on this? He knew they could not give him the help he needed.

He had to figure it out himself. As for presenting the Great Magician to the Dark Lord's army? Even a walk through the fresh country air could not seem to shake his puny self into inspiration. It all felt so impossible.

Harry knew that people often looked for a sign or wonder to be a miracle.

But it can also be a disaster.

You just have to look close enough into the ruin, to see there just might be something wondrous in it.

For that is the big lesson of this Christmas tale. Look closer. Look farther. Look within. See as much as you can from as many angles as you can, for in the long run, you and I shall be the better for it. Harry needed to look harder.

After a sleepless Friday night, Harry, as scheduled, joined the final rehearsal of the nativity pageant on the town hall stage on Saturday morning. It was always held on the green on Christmas Eve, but the final rehearsal was conducted indoors so the shoppers could shop.

Harry was a shepherd for the fifth year in a row. Honey was an angel for the fourth

75

year. As far as Harry was concerned, Honey was never an angel except for during the Christmas pageant. The rest of the time, she was an annoying know-it-all. Harry did not like her, but every day, he tried to love her. Most days, he failed.

For the first time, little Harvest Moon, who had turned two, was playing a lamb in the manger. A real infant was used every year to play the baby. Little Harvest was bummed because when he was young enough to play the role, he cried too much and had to be replaced.

This year, he was going to be the best lamb he could be in the Christmas pageant.

Not that he fully understood what that meant.

And even in his darkest hour, as Harry stood with his staff and shepherd's robe of sheets, he was proud of his mom. Every year, as the director, she pulled the pageant together. Mary Moon was always cool about it. She kept her head. She could even be funny. He felt a little sad for her, for over the years, the pageant seemed to become less and less important as the bylaws of Mayor Kligore's town grew stronger.

The pageant used to have words and scenes and everything. Now, it was just Mary, Joseph, and the baby Jesus sitting in the gazebo, singing a bunch of songs. But they were still great songs, and there was still the Great Magician sleeping in a humble animal feeding trough. All the noise in the world could not drown out the music of the spheres on the town green on Christmas Eve.

At his mom's direction, the choral director, Mrs. Middlemarch, who was also the editor of the town paper, cued the angels. It was a big chorus this year, amounting to about forty girls and boys. They sang, almost on key, the classic Christmas song—

Shepherds, why this jubilee?
Why your joyous strains prolong?
What the gladsome tidings be,
Which inspire your heav'nly song?

Gloria in excelsis Deo.
Gloria in excelsis Deo.

Harry watched as Reverend Allen entered the town hall. His face was flushed and crimson red. As the rehearsal song concluded, Reverend Allen took Harry's mom to the side of the stage and whispered something to her.

Harry watched his mother's brow furrow. Her hand crushed the stage directions into a little ball of crumpled paper. Composing herself, she returned to the stage to address the several hundred people there. "We will be moving our pageant this year, at the request of Mayor Kligore," she announced. "It seems that the Mayor would like us to move the event to the church basement. It appears that the planning board voted the pageant as too religious for a public town square. I'm so sorry." Everyone in the town hall groaned. Harry groaned also, but it was difficult to keep his mind on the pageant.

As Harry and his family walked across the town green, Harry looked over at the Sleepy Hollow Magic Shoppe shrouded in darkness. His heart sunk as he thought of his dear teacher slowly being snuffed out by the dark veil hanging over the shop. He had to think of something.

On the ride home, Harvest Moon wept. "I wanted to play the baby!"

Harry Moon patted his two-year-old brother's back.

"But that was because you were a bit of a crybaby," said Honey sympathetically.

"Now, I won't even be a lamb!"

"But you'll still be a lamb. Just now in the basement," Harry said. But Harvest could not be consoled. He put his tiny face in his tiny hands and sobbed at the seeming injustice.

"Isn't there anything we can do, Mom?" Honey asked.

"Make the best of it," Mary Moon said.

79

"But we have to fight!" Harry said. "We'll raise money against this!"

"It is not the money," said Mary Moon. "It's a silly five-dollar permit that the town refuses to issue. It's the idea of a real baby and a real celebration. Sleepy Hollow doesn't like it. It's not *Halloweeny* enough for the by-laws."

"But it is not Halloweeny even a little bit. It is just the pure thing!" said Harry, flustered. "Can't we have just one pure thing in this blasted town?"

"Christmas Eve is on Monday. Town Hall closes at noon for the holiday. If you don't want that pageant in the basement, then think of what we can do," said Mary, challenging her son.

That afternoon, there was a great celebration in the underground conference room of the Grotto at Folly Farm. The corrupt head of the planning board, Judas Octavius, tore the pageant permit in two and handed it to Lady

Dra Dra.

The Imperial Captain of Dragons, in a snake-green wig, slithered across the marble floor of the conference room. She threw the permit into the fire of the stone hearth.

Before the torn permit even reached the blazing logs, it flared. Two flames, rising in the chimney, consumed the paper like a fiery monster. Normally so stoic, Mayor Maximus Kligore danced a little jig in front of the fire. There was nothing ironic in that dance of his. He had set Christmas back once again. He was in a state of utter bliss.

81

82

Verse Six

CREEPY THOR

Harry could hardly think. He knew it was up to him to save his teacher, Samson Dupree. Was there a way to save the outdoor pageant as well?

Angerly clinching his fist, he simply wanted to tear down the door of the Sleepy Hollow Magic Shoppe. The canceling of the outdoor Christmas pageant only fueled his passion. He stood on the sidewalk outside the magic store with Declan Dickinson as they discussed what options Harry had up his magic sleeve.

"What are we gonna do, man?" Declan asked. "How are you going to get him here? We gonna pull his beard down from the clouds and drag him to the door?"

"Stop talking kindergarten, man. I am pretty sure that the Great Magician doesn't have a beard," Harry said.

"Then, where is he?" Declan said as he walked with Harry across the green.

Harry thought, looking up to the sky, looking for inspiration.

"Rabbit says I have to dig deep and watch for the sign," Harry said. Declan sighed as the parody of "I'll Be Home for Christmas" blasted over the speakers.

I'll be cloned for Christmas,
there'll be three of me;
One to work, and one to shop,
and one just to par-tee!

Christmas Eve, I'm certain,
I won't be alone;
I'll be home for Christmas,
or else I'll send a clone!

Declan looked at Harry as if he had been struck by lightning. "There is your sign! Right there, in that stupid Christmas parody. You are going to clone my drone with your magic. We are going to attack the magic shop with an army of helidrones until it coughs up your teacher!"

So it was decided that the very next night, the Good Mischief Team would wreck helidrone havoc on the Sleepy Hollow Magic Shoppe. Declan would bring his drone that was not quite yet his Christmas present, and Harry would bring his magic. Together, with the other guys, the Good Mischief Team would take the shop back.

They would tear down the walls of the store

if they had to in order to save Samson.

Later that day, "What Child is This" played on the little portable speaker in the kitchen of the Moon home on Nightingale Lane.

What Child is this,
Who, laid to rest
On Mary's lap, is sleeping?
Whom Angels greet with anthems sweet,
While shepherds watch are keeping?
So bring Him incense, gold, and myrrh,
Come Peasant, King to own Him,
The King of Kings salvation brings,
Let loving hearts enthrone Him.

"What kind of tree are you thinking we should bring home?" Harry asked his mother as they stood in the kitchen. She put money in his pocket for the purchase.

"You're thirteen, and you're headed to high school next fall," said Mary Moon, trying to be cheerful despite the news of the canceling of the pageant in the square. "You'll know which tree is best to make our Christmas merry!"

"Okay," said Harry, tentatively. He looked unconvinced.

"Just let the Christmas spirit move you. Let the tree pick you." Mary Moon turned back to the kitchen island. She placed the twelfth layer on the Christmas cake. "And before I forget, will you please invite Samson Dupree for Christmas dinner this year? I worry about him so. We are probably the closest thing to family he knows."

87

Harry took the frosting knife and smoothed the delicious final layer of icing at the top of the cake.

"Umm, ummm he . . . he might be on vacation."

"Where?" Mary asked.

"The black forest," Harry answered.

"The black forest? In Austria? Invite him

anyway. Two o'clock, like always."

As Harry left the house with his dad, he thought about the tree he would get at the Treeodin Christmas Tree Fair. But his heart was elsewhere.

I am going to bring down that store! I'll show those ghouls the power of the Great Magician!

Harry's dad pulled the minivan onto the Treeodin Tree Fair parking lot. As the fair was controlled by We Drive By Night, it was abundant in its Halloween parodies.

There were trees painted orange and pink and blue. Others were flocked with sparkles. There were few regular green firs or pines. And of course, the music was from the We Drive By Night approved playlist—

Joy to the world!
The teacher's dead!
We barbecued her head!
What happened to her body?
We flushed it down the potty!

And round and round it goes,
And round and round it goes . . .

"Picking the right tree is an art, kiddo," John Moon said. "I'm counting on you, Harrold, to pick wisely." Harry nodded and split off from his dad who was off to get garlands cut for the inside staircase. Families were out shopping

for their last minute trees. It was but two days before Christmas. Hearing his mom's voice in his head, Harry called out into the rows of trees, both painted and not.

"Tree, are you there?" Harry called. "Moon family tree, can you hear me?"

"What the devil are you doing?" asked a voice.

90

Harry turned to see a creepy tall kid with dark eyes and a white goth face. He was bent over an animal pen. He wore a beat-up brown leather bomber jacket with a silver lightning bolt on the front pocket. This was Thor Treeodin, better known at school as simply "creepy Thor." His parents owned the tree farm.

"I'm looking for a Christmas tree," said Harry.

Thor Treeodin stood, his pale face staring at Harry. "So, you thought you would call for it?" Thor asked, his mouth grim, his eyes surly. "Like, wow. What's that about?"

Harry did not want to tell Thor that his mom suggested to him that he let the tree pick him. *I don't want the creepy Thor to think I talk with my mommy.*

"Why not?" Harry said, thinking fast on his feet. "I read somewhere that plants can feel, too."

"They can," said Thor, staring down at Harry. "But they got to be A-L-I-V-E. These trees are D-E-A-D."

91

"You have some live ones, then?" Harry asked.

"We do," said Thor. Harry was surprised. *What? Live trees?* Harry looked around and saw that Thor had been feeding some goats in a pen. The pen was clean and the feeding trough held fresh grain. Harry watched as Thor leaned into the pen and petted one of the goats. His touch was gentle and affectionate. Harry was surprised at the creepy Thor's tenderness. "They're kinda hard to find," Thor replied. "There are just a few. I'll take you to them."

Harry wanted to get away from him.

"Aww, you don't need to do that, just point me in the right direction," Harry said.

"I said I'll take you there," repeated Thor, sternly. "Don't want you wandering around our property."

Harry followed the tall leather-clad Viking. Thor Treeodin kept to himself at middle school. Thor preferred to keep it that way, and he might just fight you to protect his space. So Harry was a little taken aback when Thor opened up a conversation with him.

"You like nature?" Thor said. At first, Harry was not sure what to say. Then, he decided he would just be himself.

"Oh yeah," replied Harry.

They passed an old, weather-beaten barn toward the back end of the property where the tree rows seemed to disappear. "Let me show you something," Thor said.

Thor walked over to the barn door and slid it open. Harry was slightly afraid, but as he neared, he was impressed to see the barn full of stables. There were cows, horses, goats, sheep, and even a few llamas.

"This is the winter barn for the McCracken Farm. I watch over the animals when the McCrackens are in Florida for the winter."

"Wow," Harry said. He was impressed, for the barn was very tidy and clean. "That's a lot of animals to feed."

93

"Almost sixty in here, but they behave. I like to get them out in little groups for some fresh air like the goats you saw back there."

"Wow," said Harry.

"Yeah, but I don't keep 'em out too long else they might freeze. Anyway, thought you might like seeing 'em since you like nature."

Harry watched as Thor pulled an apple from a feedbag. He held up the fruit to a black gelding who took the apple.

"Here, you give one to Happy, that's the sister to this gelding." Thor handed Harry an apple. Harry walked over to a brown horse and palmed the apple for the horse to nibble. And Happy did. Harry could feel Thor's eyes upon him, subtlety judging him as if in some kind of initiation rite.

"Happy likes you," said Thor.

"Why wouldn't she?" Harry said with a laugh. "I just palmed her an apple."

The two boys walked out of the barn. Thor secured the door. Harry continued to follow Thor beyond the barn until they reached an area that held a dozen or so trees, their roots in painted red tins.

"These are the living trees," said Thor. "Once in a while, not too often, we have a crunchy-granola customer who wants to keep the tree after Christmas. So I potted these for them."

"So what do you do with these after Christmas?" said Harry.

"If you keep them in these here tins, they won't grow much more. You could put it on the patio, or if you want it to grow, you could replant it in your yard."

"What a great idea," said Harry. He looked over at the trees and then walked about them looking for one with a nice symmetry. There were pine and spruce, as well. On his second look, Harry believed he had found the tree. It was well proportioned with a nice flare to the ground. Yet, it was not much taller than Harry. He knew his mother liked a tree with more height to fit the great room. And he knew Honey would have a conniption. But this tree seemed to be reaching out to him.

"This one here. What about this one?" asked Harry.

"I think that spruce has your name on it, Harry Moon."

95

"Thanks, Thor. This tree says a lot about the Christmas Spirit."

"What do you mean, Crunchy?" asked Thor. His mouth remained grim, but there was some sparkle in his eyes.

"That the Christmas Spirit is A-L-I-V-E."

The two boys put the tree onto a wooden wagon. Thor pulled the wagon as Harry pushed it. Thor said he thought the Christmas season was too commercial. He told Harry that neither he nor his family celebrated it, but that Christmas was a good time to make some extra money before the long winter set in.

At the register, Harry paid for the tree with the money his mother had given him. Thor helped him wagon it to the van where his dad waited.

"Interesting tree, Harry. You do know your mother likes a tall Christmas tree for the holidays."

"Why not, Dad? She likes me," Harry said. "It's almost as short as me."

Harry observed Thor smiling as he discussed the tree with his father. The three guys loaded the tree onto the roof of the van and bungeed it tight.

You would have thought it was Christmas the way the Moon family ran to the front door of the house, all excited. Of course, it was Christmas. Well, almost. Half Moon barked at the new tree as he licked the sap. Honey Moon giggled as she held open the front door so it wouldn't slam shut. Harvest ran in circles in his bib overalls screaming, "Tree, tree, tree!"

"Hmmm," Mary Moon said, staring at the tiny thing as Harry and his dad shuffled into the house, half carrying, half dragging the potted tree toward the great room.

Sensing this was the time to curry favor with her mother, Honey said, "That is one puny tree, Harry Moon. What in the world were you thinking, brother? I waited all year for this tree.

Santa won't even be able to find it for our present drop."

"Don't send ta' tree back, Mommy!" said Harvest jumping off the sofa and running across the great room. He hugged his mother's legs. "It's just my size!"

Mary Moon smiled. She sighed as her toddler held on to her legs for dear life. "Then I will love it all the more for it will remind me of you," Mary said as she squeezed Harvest right back.

John Moon strung the colored lights first. Later, the boxes were brought from the attic. The Moon family hung the bright, shiny ornaments.

After dinner, Harry quietly walked into the great room to see the Christmas tree all lit up in the dark room.

He turned and closed the door behind him. Alone with the tree, Harry took a step back and looked it over. The lights were hung nicely on the green limbs. An ornament hung from every branch. He saw the little wooden caboose Aunt Debbie had given him hanging prominently at the front. He saw the cotton swab elf he made in first grade hanging from another.

After studying the tree for a while, he realized that he was not alone.

He heard shallow breathing from across the room. He turned and saw, in the glow of the tree, Harvest and Half Moon sitting very quietly in the dark next to one another on the sofa. Harvest petted Half. They stared at the tree, perfectly content.

At that moment, Harry wished he had his cell so he could take a picture. *I guess,* he thought, *I will just have to remember this another way.*

"Whatcha' doin', big guy?" asked Harry.

"Hangin'," replied Harvest.

"Want me to put on some carols?" asked Harry.

"I tink they are already on."

Harry smiled. He walked over to the sofa.

"Can I join you guys?"

Harvest looked at Half Moon to obtain the

dog's approval. Half Moon stared at Harvest.

"Sure, Harry," answered Harvest.

Harry sat next to his brother.

The three of them stared across the dark room at the sparkling tree.

"Can you hear the carols now, Harry?" asked Harvest.

101

Harry snuggled into the couch with his brother and the hound as they watched the lights.

Harry listened.

There was not a sound, yet there was music everywhere.

"Yep, Harvest, I believe I can," replied Harry with a smile.

102

Verse Seven

THE ATTACK OF THE DRONES

There were too many shoppers on Magic Row not to attract attention, so the Good Mischief Team met behind the store. They did not want to be interrupted by tourist hounds. Harry, Hao, Declan, and Bailey climbed up and sat in the trees on the other side of the alley, looking at the back windows of the magic store.

Above them, from the tree's dark branches, over a hundred eyes stared out from the barren winter branches. These were the drones created by Harry's magic. They had been "cloned" from a small sliver of the cyan-blue wing of Declan's Christmas gift. The guys had dipped each drone nose into a mandragora stew, a recipe found in Samson's grimoire, a magic-manual gift to Harry on his thirteenth birthday. Now fifty drones hovered in the crowns of the many trees, humming in the low tones of bees in a summer garden, waiting for the command to attack.

"This is so radical," said Hao. "Just tell me when we can have at it!"

"Once the noses of the drones crack the magic store," said Harry. He held a sword of light in his power hand. "We are right behind."

"Just tell us when," said Bailey. His light sword

shivered in his grasp.

"On three, for we have to act as one," said Harry. "Only teamwork gives us the shot at this."

"Ready when you are, Captain," said Declan from the very top of the maple tree.

High in the bleak elm, absent of leaves, Harry whispered softly:

O Ancient of Days,
Hear our praise,
Do not let our word go unheard,
Fly these drones like the thunderbird.

O Ancient of Days!
Hear our praise,
Break the spell upon this wall,
Until there is no charm at all.

With a larger voice, Harry commanded his friends by his count. "One . . . two . . . three!"

With a single voice of fellowship, the cheer

came through the trees with a resounding, "A B R A C A D A B R A!"

The one hundred eyes shot through the alley. There was a tremendous rush of light, as bright and varied as the starry light Harry glimpsed in Samson's eyes.

Like speeding arrows, the charmed drones penetrated the brick wall of the back of the store. The light flashed across the alley and disappeared into the brick. There was a tremendous roar from within, like a great monster in the death throes.

It was a ghastly howling.

And then just as quickly as the howling had begun, the sound died.

The bricks fell away and standing from ground to ceiling was a dark mass of creatures. There was a Merlin action figure gone berserk, gnashing its teeth. There was a wooden Gepetto, his spectacles as big as windows, his work apron as black as belladonna petals. The giant Gepetto shouted at the boys.

"Come and get some, my children!" the giant cried. The voice was raspy like the deep, disturbing rhythm of a rattlesnake.

This was a call to arms. The four boys jumped down from the trees. In the alley, they brought the tips of their light swords together. Gripping the handles tightly, Harry led the boys

107

in the second command. "One . . . two . . . three," Harry said.

"A B R A C A D A B R A!" the fellowship replied.

The light came forth from the collected apex of swords, running down the blades to the pommels gripped in their hands.

"Come an' get it, kids!" shouted the Merlin monster toy. His cowl was over his head. His snake-yellow eyes peered through the darkness in his face. He was no longer the pint-sized action figure but a hideous wraith as tall as Gepetto.

The two giants stood on each side of the building.

"Soups on!" shouted the Merlin figure.

As he commanded, a flood of spiders, ants, and snakes spilled out of the mouth of darkness where the door had once been.

"Don't be afraid of the dark," said Harry as if to convince himself.

"Don't be afraid of the dark!" the other boys joined in the chant of the Good Mischief Team.

His sparkling sword gripped with both hands, Harry carried it forward as if it was a giant candlestick. The black spiders and black serpents climbed into his boots.

Harry continued with his cry.

"Don't be afraid of the dark!" he said.

"Don't be afraid of the dark!" the boys replied.

A black spider leaped into Bailey's mouth as he approached the dark supernatural wall held by Merlin and Gepetto. Bailey spit out the critter in fear and revulsion and howled.

"Why are we not supposed to be afraid of the dark?" Bailey exclaimed, his spirit withering.

"For there is always a light!" Harry shouted. "And we are the light!"

Harry ran toward the monstrous Gepetto. He swung his saber at the demon's leg. The light cut right through the pants of the toymaker ogre.

"Your light means nothing," shouted the toymaker. "For I shall snuff it out!"

110

"Go ahead and try, monster!" shouted Harry. Harry ran into the dark shroud of the store. Declan, Hao, and Bailey followed behind.

The store was completely empty. There were no shelves. There was no counter. There was no Samson.

Harry looked above him at the net of Magic 8 balls. They had grown as tarnished as cannon balls. They winked their pronouncement at him.

"No. No. No," read the magic balls.

"What have you done with Samson?" Harry

shouted. Reaching up with his light sword, Declan slashed at the net. The Magic 8 balls fell heavily on the boys with crushing blows. Bailey and Hao screamed as the magic balls now winked, "Ha. Ha. Ha."

"Give Samson back to us!" Harry shouted.

Declan and Hao slashed their light sabers at the dark walls, but there seemed to be nothing there but the somber, infinite air. Yet, their light sabers must have unleashed something.

111

"Look!" Harry shouted.

As the boys slashed recklessly, the silver castle that was the centerpiece of the store began to materialize on the floor. It now looked as dark and gloomy as Sleeping Beauty's castle.

But thorn and ivy did not cover it. It was overwhelmed by a creeping darkness. At every rampart and tower nested a crowd of spiders. Harry looked through the tiny open drawbridge. Within the small and dark castle, Harry saw Samson's shrunken and withering body. He lay on the floor as if a body for funereal viewing. Harry's heart leaped at the sight of his teacher, now the size of a thumb.

Samson coughed out, "Help me. Help me, Harry!" The tiny body struggled to sit up in the tiny room. The small Samson looked directly at Harry. "Hurry, Harry!" he whispered.

Harry stood. He moved away from the castle so that his swing could carry the muscle of his heft. He raised his light sword.

With one strain of his back, Harry tore the sword into the castle. Part of the ramparts exploded into dust as Harry's blade cut through the brick. Harry kneeled and reached into the castle. The buttresses surrounding the tiny magic shop were still strong. Samson was too encased for him to even place a finger near him for the dear guardian was not much bigger than a sliver.

"Hit the sides, men, he is in the very middle of the tiny fortress!" Harry shouted to his brothers in the Good Mischief Team. Bailey, Declan, and Hao surrounded the other sides of the fortress.

"On three!" Harry commanded." One . . . two . . . three!" Harry lowered his hand and the three other guys cut at the ramparts as they shouted in unison, "A B R A C A D A B R A!"

Their silver hilts cut away at the Modbot structure. When the dust cleared, only a single tower remained. The four guys, surrounding the remnant, leaned into it. There lay the tiny Samson in the midst of the lone tower. Declan looked behind him. Everywhere, there were eyes staring at them all, as if ready to pounce. Harry looked as well. There were Red Riding Hood and the other wizards. There were the many eyes of the spiders and snakes, looking up from the dreadful floor. They all incanted the hideous noise of the Fouling Curse—

We have a bed for Samson to lay his head,
Your teacher is as good as dead!

113

By the pricking of our thumbs,
Something wicked this way comes!

Darkness swallows light! Time to give up
*   the fight,*
Deck the halls with slime! It's
*   Christmastime!*
Once the shadow works as could,
Then the charm is firm and good!

The spiders and snakes began to scream. As the darkness attempted to lay itself over the four swords of light, a wind rose in the darkness. The swords turned as if they had an energy all their own. Indeed, the swords did. Harry and the Good Mischief Team held on to the pommels. The swords lifted into the air and whisked the guys from the trap of gloom.

In that sudden winking, a force grabbed the swords. The power drew the tips of the blades toward the back of the store. The guys yelped as they soared through the chilly gloom and through the dark shroud.

"Such swordplay is grand, but it is not the

solution to the Fouling Curse," said the voice in the alley.

The guys had fallen onto the pavement in the alley behind the store. Their light swords skittered across the thin ice of the alley. The giant Gepetto and the tremendous Merlin with the yellow eyes had vanished. Harry looked up from the pavement to see the back of the store, quiet and dark, as if nothing had just happened.

115

"The only answer is to produce the Great Magician for this fight," the voice continued. The Team looked around and could not see the source of the voice. Only Harry could see Rabbit sitting in the elm tree.

"Your drones and swords are marvelous, but they will not work in this arena," the voice called.

"But how?" Harry called out to Rabbit in the branches.

"It is all before you," Rabbit said.

And Harry knew immediately that was Rabbit's exit. He looked up to the barren limbs of the elm, and Rabbit had vanished.

"So that is the voice you are always talking about?" asked Declan.

"Yes," said Harry.

"And it directs your magic?" Declan looked sideways at Bailey.

116

"It is the voice of Rabbit. He guides me," said Harry.

"Now what?" asked Bailey. He stood up. He picked up his sword.

Harry stood as well. "We regroup. Apparently, the answer is right in front of us."

Verse Eight

A GHOSTLY MEMORY

Back in his bedroom, Harry tried to sleep. He thought if he could, he would be able to come up with some answer to the Fouling Curse and save Samson by morning. He replayed the last few days in his head, but there appeared to be no forthcoming answer that was "all before" him. To break the curse required him to produce the Great Magician. *Maybe I should just try and pull on the clouds like Declan suggested. It seems easier than any other solution.*

After a while his stomach grumbled. A sandwich might help him sleep. Then maybe the answer would come. He crept down the stairs. Harvest was a light sleeper, and Harry did not want to wake him. He walked into the front hallway and through the dining alcove. There he saw the words that were stenciled above the rim of the room. They were the virtues that Rabbit spoke often—love, joy, peace, patience, kindness, faithfulness, goodness, and gentleness.

He opened the refrigerator and pulled out bread and lettuce and ham and cheese and pickles and mayo. He did a pretty good job of stacking those goodies together into one massive ham and cheese. The kitchen light was so eye-squinting bright that he decided to take

118

his midnight snack into the great room.

He would watch the latest Patriot's game, which he had missed last Sunday. But once he got into the room, he saw the living tree in the corner and decided to light it. Like Harvest and Half Moon earlier, he just sat on the sofa in the quiet. The tree was beautiful. It was the one thing he had gotten right. They could set it out on the patio and bring it in every Christmas. After a few bites of his sandwich, he went over to the red-painted tin to check the soil. He reached under the tree and found that the soil was moist. His dad must have watered it once they finished decorating it.

119

"You like nature, don't you?" said a voice in the room. Harry looked around. At first, he thought it was the tree.

"Are you talking to me?" Harry said, staring at the spruce branches.

Of course, there was no answer. But the voice spoke again as Harry headed back to the sofa.

"So you like nature?" the voice asked again. It was the same question that Thor Treeodin had asked him earlier. But the voice was young, like a child's.

He realized the voice was coming from a memory he had long forgotten. There was Thor Treeodin, standing before him at the petting zoo in the town green. Thor was maybe seven. He was tall, even then. He wore his signature

120

brown leather jacket. There was a large pony with a saddle. Harry stood in front of the pony in the middle of the Treeodin Petting Zoo.

"Yes, I do like nature," Harry said. He had been crying. There were tear tracks staining his face.

"Blue," said the young Thor. "She's a gentle one. I tamed her myself. She won't hurt you. I promise you, Harry. And I will hold on to the reins for you until you are ready. If you like nature, well, you are gonna love Blue."

Harry looked up at Thor. The tall boy made a step with his hands. "Just step on my hands, and I'll lift ya' up. You ain't too heavy for me," said Thor. Harry put his left foot in Thor's hands, and Thor lifted him up on the saddle.

Harry recalled that day as he sat on the sofa, looking at the ornaments and lights on the tree. It was a great ride. He even gave the reins back to Thor. Those were the days when the Treeodin Petting Zoo came four or five times a year to the town green.

Harry could even remember the times that he brought Honey to the zoo. Thor helped her onto her first pony too. Harry remembered Thor showing him the other animals. It was a bit foggy, but Harry remembered back to a time when he was ten and saw a real-life llama for the first time. It was strange that Harry remembered all of it, but he never really got to know Thor in middle school.

122

He was a loner, and Harry never shared homeroom with him. Then Thor seemed to withdraw even further into himself. He got into some fights and even got suspended once.

There was a reason he was named "creepy Thor." He seemed to creep about on the sides of the school halls and never really engaged with any of the other kids.

After he finished his ham and cheese, Harry felt his stomach working overtime. He punched up some pillows and lay down on the cozy sofa. It felt plush and warm, and of course, there were the sparkling lights of the tree.

Before Harry knew it, he opened his eyes to the ornaments with morning light slanting through the window. Harvest was jumping on his chest, and Half Moon was lapping his face.

"Is it Christmas yet?" Harry said.

"No, silly! No, no, no! You fell asleep in front of the tree," Harvest said. "But Santa is coming tonight! Tonight!"

"Don't jinx the magic, buddy," Harry said.

133

"Don't say don't to me!" Harvest said as he jumped on his older brother.

124

Verse Nine

WHEN HEAVEN AND NATURE SING

It was still very early that Christmas Eve
morning. The sun was just rising over the
Sleepy Hollow treetops. Harry did not have

the time to ride his bike all the way down Mayflower Road to the Treeodin Tree Fair, so he decided to make his way there on the Astral Road as his friend had taught him. He quickly dressed in boots, parka, and scarf as it was cold and windy. By calling on a special incantation Samson gave him, Harry shrunk down to a size smaller than an atom. This was the same magic Harry had used earlier when he disappeared in thin air from Declan Dickinson's rooftop, moving from one place to another by traveling within the space between the tiniest of particles.

To anyone not familiar with Samson's, and now Harry's, magic, it would appear that Harry simply vanished in his bedroom. But if you could look microscope-close, that being very, very close, and were able to place Harry under a super magnifying lens, you would find him only slightly larger than the nucleus of an atom. By becoming momentarily porous, Harry flew in between that minuscule space where protons and electrons encircle the atom's nucleus. And since he was in a world beyond time, Harry Moon flew speedily through billions and billions of atoms as if he himself were of ghostly substance.

He was a thirteen-year-old kid, traveling through a world that we cannot see with our sense of eyesight. When Harry arrived at the Treeodin Tree Fair, he grew back into his normal self. He ground himself quickly into the snow and looked around for Thor. He saw him leading horses from the McCracken barn into some outdoor fencing where the horses would have room to walk.

127

"Hey, Thor!" Harry cried out as he ran to the barn door. Harry should have been more subdued, but it was early, and he had not even had his breakfast. "Thor, I need your help," he called as he got closer to him. Thor wore his leather jacket and a hat with ear flaps because the morning air was frosty. Harry could tell that he startled Thor when Thor's eyes opened as wide as silver dollars.

"Hey, where did you come from?" Thor looked around. "I didn't see anyone pull up. What are you doing here so early?"

"I'm here because I need your help," Harry said.

Thor looked surprised. "How could I possibly help you?" Thor's eyebrows wrinkled. The horse whinnied.

"Last night, I was thinking back to all those years that you and your family had the petting zoo in the green. Well, I thought how great it would be to have a petting zoo today, on Christmas Eve. You could bring all the animals, and they could watch on the green with all the people for Christmas to come."

"Huh? Have you gone loco, Harry?"

"No, I am completely sane, Thor! The town has shut down the Christmas pageant, but that doesn't mean the animals from the manger couldn't show up!"

"You mean like all the animals from the barn?" asked Thor.

"Like a whole parade of animals!" Harry

said. "It is Christmas Eve after all, and it would be just like the song, "Joy to the World." Harry cleared his throat and sang a few bars to the confused-looking Thor:

And Heaven and nature sing,
And Heaven and nature sing,
And Heaven, and Heaven, and nature sing!

Harry looked at Thor. "Listen man, I remember when I was a scared little kid, and you showed me how I should not be frightened of your horse Blue."

129

"Blue?" said Thor. His eyes widened at the thought of her. "I do remember Blue. Gosh, she was a beauty an' a gentle one, that's for sure."

"She was. She was the very first horse I ever rode. I was a crying, sniveling kid, and you showed me how not to be afraid. You showed me to love nature."

Harry had to do a lot of convincing to get Thor to see his vision. But, eventually, Thor did catch it. No one had ever been so convincing with him. It was as if Harry Moon had known his heart. And while Thor may have felt anxious around people and stayed clear of them, he listened to Harry. He listened because Harry regarded him in the place where his true heart lived. Thor might have been known by most kids as the creepy Thor. But in reality, Thor was the creep who had a soft heart for animals.

"You know why I am gonna help?" Thor said. "Because you sang that song. Cause you sang that Heaven and nature song. I liked that. We aren't church folk, but I do believe if people only could see how beautiful nature is, this world would be a lot better off."

Thor and Harry would have to convince Thor's dad that the last minute petting zoo made sense. Odin Treeodin was a burly, brash horseman. He had long silver hair that he wore in a ponytail. When Harry saw Odin Treeodin on the street, he simply dismissed him as some biker with low-humming brain waves. But Harry was surprised by how well-spoken Odin Treeodin was. "So you fellas are wanting to do something inspiring like

Francesco of Assisi?" asked Odin Treeodin.

"I don't know what Francesco of Assisi did," said Thor.

"He staged the first nativity, that's what he did," said Odin.

Odin then told the boys the story of how the young monk saw all the animals grazing in the fields and mountains. He had the idea to reenact the story of the Christmas birth. "He even found a mother in the village of Assisi who had just given birth to be in his story." Odin became animated with the two boys. "It was said that on Christmas night all the animals came 'round the mother and child, and it was such a heavenly moment, you could hear the angels sing. That was the first manger in the year twelve hundred and ever since, for over eight hundred years, people have been putting sheep and cows in the Christmas story with the mother and child. So you want to do that?"

"Yes, sir," said Harry. "That's exactly what we want to do."

131

"It's just like the carol, Dad," said Thor. "Like I was tellin' Harry. *And Heaven and nature sing.*"

Harry watched as Odin Treeodin's expression grew bright with mischief. "So we would have to get a permit from Kligore's office first thing this morning for the petting zoo. They close early. You know what's funny about getting this permit? Heck, how many years, son, have we gotten that town permit?"

"As long as I can remember, Dad," said Thor.

"It is really going to tick off Mayor Kligore. I say let Christmas be! Not everything in the world is meant to be *Halloweeny!*" Harry watched as Odin Treeodin slapped his son's back. Sweet astonishment flooded Thor's eyes as his dad hugged him. Harry had the feeling that it had been a while since Thor had gotten a hug like that. "Let's go mess with Kligore's Christmas."

In the early morning mist, Harry was encouraged not only by the affection between father and son but that this plan might just work. Harry sat in the backseat of the pickup truck while Odin drove and Thor sat shotgun. They still had to secure the permit to stage the animal parade in the public green. It would take some clever maneuvering not to attract attention with the last minute request. "I'll do the talking here, guys," said Odin. "I've known the permit clerk for years. Even before either of you were born."

"Why did you stop doing the petting zoos?" asked Harry.

133

"Honestly, son, we just got tired of the pressure. The planning committee kept begging us to dress up the goats as vampires and put headless horsemen on the ponies. I said to them, 'Where are the kids supposed to sit if the ponies have headless riders?' They just looked at me as if I was nuts! Then you know what they said?" Odin let out a belly laugh.

"What was that, sir?" asked Harry. He liked how fun Odin was. Odin Treeodin reminded Harry of his own dad.

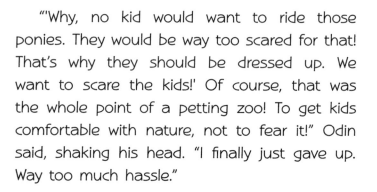

"'Why, no kid would want to ride those ponies. They would be way too scared for that! That's why they should be dressed up. We want to scare the kids!' Of course, that was the whole point of a petting zoo! To get kids comfortable with nature, not to fear it!" Odin said, shaking his head. "I finally just gave up. Way too much hassle."

"Then why are you helping us out now?" Harry said, including Thor in the "us."

134

"Cause our animals aren't dressing up!" said Odin, happily. "And besides, it's Christmas!"

Treeodin pulled the truck up to the town hall and into one of the Sleepy Hollow visitor parking spaces in front of the door. The town green was quiet. The Clock Tower chimed nine bells. As Harry stepped out of the truck, he had a queasy feeling. He looked across the green at the Sleepy Hollow Magic Shoppe. Over the darkened door, someone had hung a sign. Closed for the Season. Harry was sure it was someone from Mayor Kligore's office. A pall had settled over the town square. Soon, there would be the shoppers out for their last-minute shopping. But without the shoppers, the town felt very empty, especially for Christmas Eve.

Odin Treeodin slapped Harry on the back. "Town feels creepy, huh? You feel it too? I'm telling you, something's just not right about this place. Absolutely no Christmas vibe. Well, we will change all that tonight." Harry could not believe that Thor's dad could sense his feelings. He was suddenly buoyed out of his queasiness. "Come on boys, let's teach this town how nature and Heaven sing!"

135

Odin climbed the steps, two at a time. Harry and Thor followed him. "Wow, your dad is rockin'," Harry whispered to Thor.

Thor smiled. "Why do you say that?"

"'Cause he really listens. I mean, your dad really listens," said Harry.

"Yeah. He's good that way," said Thor, a

sense of affection and pride appearing in his eyes for his father.

"Can I ask you why you drop letters from your words and use slang like 'ain't?'" Harry said.

"It's part of the act. Dad says people expect us crunchy-granola hicks who sell trees to be illiterate. I start talking, and they kind of feel sorry for us and leave us alone. *Ain't* is a great social blockade. When they hear it, they drop their engagement. They leave me alone."

Harry continued up the steps. He realized he had his own prejudice. Thor had never ever done anything bad to him. And yet, Harry had always kept his distance. He could not understand why. He vowed to change that from that moment forward.

Harry wondered if the town would issue a permit for the square at such a last minute. Thor's dad seemed to be fairly certain. And if boisterousness had anything to do with it, Odin would certainly have his way.

As it was practically a holiday, the town hall was quiet as the three walked down the long corridor to the town clerks at the end of the hall. There were several clerk windows open that Christmas Eve morning, and they all closed at noon. There was one window open for rubbage removal permits. There was a second window open for hunting licenses. A third window was open for public permits.

"Merry Christmas, Margaret sweetheart!" Odin Treeodin shouted out as he approached the permit window. "Did you ever come by for your tree? I didn't see you!"

"Merry Christmas, Odin." Margaret was sipping on a steaming cup of hot cider and wrinkled her nose. "Of course we did! Randy came by last week and picked out a beauty. You must have missed him."

Odin walked right up to the window and leaned his arm on the shelf. "I sure did. Darn. You are two of my favorite people. Hope you got a good tree."

"We did. Thanks, Odin."

"No problem, Margaret. Listen, I know it's a little late," Odin said as he lowered his voice. "I need a little favor. The family was hoping you could issue us a permit for tonight on the green. We thought it might be fun for the town if we brought some of the animals by for the kids."

"Well, I think the kids would love that," Margaret said. "I remember when I used to bring my kids by to pet your animals when you used to do that every winter. I don't see why not." She smiled wide and tapped the keyboard. "As long as you kind of keep it simple." Margaret looked around and lowered her voice to a whisper. "You know what I mean. Halloweeny and all."

"Just a barn full of animals, Margaret. Maybe a few more than the old petting zoos?"

"Just curious," asked Margaret straightening up. "What possessed you to be thinking about this at the last minute, to be doing a petting zoo on Christmas Eve, Odin?" She poked her head through the window. "Hmm. Hello there, Harry."

"Hello, Mrs. Toledo. Merry Christmas," said Harry.

"Merry Christmas, Harry," she smiled. She returned her gaze to Odin Treeodin

"And I suppose there might be a few shepherds there as well to guide the flock?"

139

"I would reckon there most probably might be," said Odin, nodding his head while looking away.

"And might there be some angels to sing on high?" said Mrs. Toledo.

"One never knows about such things, Margaret," said Odin as he turned to Thor and Harry and winked.

"Well," she said. "I cannot say who should come and who should go to this 'pet parade'

I am hereby permitting. As all things on the green, they shall be open to the public. If a few angels happen to be in the neighborhood, well, that is their business. And I guess if a mommy with a little baby happens to show up in the gazebo, that is her business. Are you sure you want to do this?"

"I am, Margaret," said Odin. "Think it will be good for the town's soul."

140

"Well, I don't know about that, but this permit gives you the ability to bring any and all animals in the Sleepy Hollow County. How long have you been permitting with us, Odin?"

"Some twenty years now," he said. He pulled a five-dollar bill from the back pocket of his jeans as Harry and Thor watched him push it through the window.

"Then you know there is the issue of animal cleanup, and that is normally a thousand dollar deposit." She looked at him and then stuck her head out of the window to cast her gaze on the boys. Her eyes were on

fire with meaning.

Harry could not mistake the look. He had seen Mrs. Toledo give that look many times. At the birthday parties for her daughter. At Fourth of July fireworks. At church events. He looked close enough to know what the look meant. It meant, *be responsible and take care of business.*

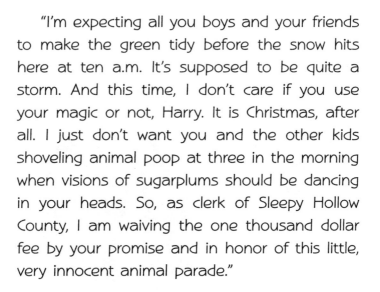

"I'm expecting all you boys and your friends to make the green tidy before the snow hits here at ten a.m. It's supposed to be quite a storm. And this time, I don't care if you use your magic or not, Harry. It is Christmas, after all. I just don't want you and the other kids shoveling animal poop at three in the morning when visions of sugarplums should be dancing in your heads. So, as clerk of Sleepy Hollow County, I am waiving the one thousand dollar fee by your promise and in honor of this little, very innocent animal parade."

"We promise, Mrs. Toledo," said Harry.

"I promise too, ma'am," added Thor.

"Then, that's good enough for the clerk's office," she replied.

BAM.

The force of the wooden stamp slamming against the permit shook the counter across all the windows. It was the stamp of the Sleepy Hollow Town Seal.

Poking her head through the window, she smiled and winked as she handed the stamped permit to Odin.

Odin winked back at her.

Later that morning, Harry and Thor presented the stamped permit to Harry's mom. When she saw the approved permit, she burst into tears. She hugged both Harry and Thor.

"Don't say don't to me!" shouted little Harvest as he came into the kitchen to join the drama.

"That's right, Harvest!" Mary Moon said. "Don't say don't to us!" She was so happy, she screamed. She studied the permit and noticed the words under the heading USAGE. "What's an animal parade?" she asked.

"Oh, it's just a little something we learned from Francesco in the little town of Assisi," Harry replied. "It's the new name of our Christmas pageant."

There was a different kind of screaming happening across town at Folly Farm.

The shouting came from the hot hearth in the Grotto three floors down. The flames whirled with color. It was the boss of all evil bosses himself.

"I told you, Kligore! This is the worst time for you to come out of the closet and hit people with this Samson thing, at Christmastime!" growled B.L. Zebub. "It's the one time of the year the people of this lousy town are good! Their awful Christmas goodness may be just enough to undo the Fouling Curse you placed on Samson!"

Kligore shook his head violently, his hair flying about right and left. "With all due respect, Mr. B.L. Zebub, step back and let me finally finish this thing once and for all. Soon, Samson Dupree will no longer be the Guardian of Harry Moon. Before the chimes of the Clock Tower ring midnight, Samson Dupree will have withered away like the Christmas holly in summer, and the Sleepy Hollow Magic Shoppe will be no more."

145

146

Verse Ten

THE STAR

Christmas morning was closer than ever. The wreaths still held dragon tails. The lamp posts surrounding the town green were still striped with fake blood and bandages.

The horseman statue, which dominated the green, remained headless.

But, if you stepped in a bit closer, you could hear the bells signaling the animal parade.

If you looked off into the distance, you could see the tender prodding of the shepherds moving the great flock of creatures along Magic Row to the gazebo. They held lanterns and staffs around the massive assembly of animals. There were sheep, goats, llamas, pigs, dogs, hounds, a few horses ridden by children, and even a few dozen cats, mostly on leashes from International Cat. Never had these animal caretakers been more focused on their jobs as they were this Christmas Eve.

Harry Moon and Harvest Moon were at the head of the flock. Harry grasped his great shepherd's staff in his power hand while his left hand held his little brother's hand.

"Man-o-man-o-man," said Harvest in his white lamb suit. His eyes jumped out of his head with excitement at the people and the

148

choir in the bandstand awaiting their arrival.

"You got that right, Harvest," Harry said as he looked back through the sea of animals. It was not his eyes but Harry's heart that jumped in his chest. He had a lump in his throat. There were little children in the throng as well, walking with their cats and dogs. At a far distance, at the back of the herd, townspeople were assembling with their own lanterns and flashlights to push away the oncoming eve.

149

And Heaven and nature sing,
And Heaven and nature sing,
And Heaven, and Heaven, and nature sing.

The final strains of the carol floated over the animals and the crowd. A beam of light flashed from the highest staff at the back of the procession. It was Harry's Dark Splitter flashlight, which Thor had tied around his broomstick. The Dark Splitter added additional light to the rear of the flock. Thor made sure that the animals did not stray as he held down the wave of animals at the back. It was

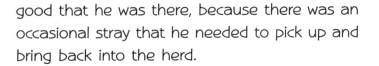

good that he was there, because there was an occasional stray that he needed to pick up and bring back into the herd.

The parade of animals was so vast that it bridged from the town green to the end of Magic Row at the Ghost Busters store. There was so much music and activity, that no one really noticed the miracle that was occurring as Thor Treeodin, carrying his broomstick, walked past the I.C. Dead People Antique Shop.

People who caught it said later that it happened as Thor approached the display window of the Sleepy Hollow Magic Shoppe. It appeared to observers of the incident that a ray of light cracked through the dark veil of the Fouling Curse enchantment that engulfed Samson's shop.

It was not much more than a twinkle, but it was light, nonetheless. It burst through the web and weave of the dark charm like a rocket on Fourth of July. It exploded with the force of a holiday firework. For the gloomy curtain that had enshrouded the ancient wizard for so long was now rising to a glorious second act.

While the songs from the green were festive and the nativity in the gazebo was lovely, there was something else that shattered the curse. For behind a beat-up bomber jacket, the long-dead, bitter heart of creepy Thor was beginning to beat in a silent cadence to the music.

No more let sins and sorrows grow,
Nor thorns infest the ground;
He comes to make His blessings flow,
Far as the curse is found,
Far as the curse is found,
Far as, far as, the curse is found.

161

Inside the shop, the silver castle glimmered under the single strand of Christmas lights that hung upon the back wall. On the shelves, the guardians of magic sat silently, from the kindly Gepetto to Merlin, Gandalf, and Dumbledore. In the net of Magic 8 balls, each globe turned and winked with a floating YES.

If you didn't blink, you could observe the dragon tails of Lady Dra Dra's spell transform into fragrant green balsam wood. The magic shop door with the small oval window swung open as if by magic.

And it was magic.

For it was Christmastime, after all.

All good stories of the season hold onto their magic for it is the season of enchantment. Even in a town where every day is Halloween night, Christmas came that very evening with a bit of a flurry and a shout.

Through the now open door of the magic shop, edged in the frame of the silver Modbot castle, gingerly and cautiously stepped the one who had come to save Sleepy Hollow from itself. Standing in the doorway and blinking, as if he had just awakened from a long slumber, Samson looked out toward the green. A little smile teasing at the corners of his mouth, he steadied himself against the doorframe as he saw the commotion of shepherds and animals moving down Main Street. His heart, just now emerging from a witching spell, was lighting up once again with joy and gratitude.

Like the Fouling Curse, that Guardian's heart, too, was witnessing the Great Magician. For the Great Magician and his deep magic can best be seen in the selfless love between one to another. And unbeknownst to him, Harry Moon had shown such love to Thor Treeodin, or as those who were ignorant of such love called him, creepy Thor. And, in turn, Thor had returned that love to the people of Sleepy Hollow with his selfless parade of animals. The Great Magician had indeed shown up after all.

153

While the shoppers were at home with their families, the green took on the beautiful life found in nature, in the sheep, goats, horses, cows, llamas, and yes, even in the shepherds guarding the flock or the angels who just happened to drop by.

The animals and shepherds encircled the white-painted gazebo. Harry sang with the

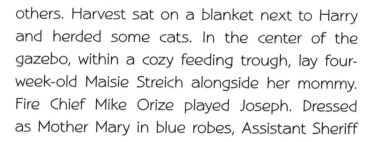

others. Harvest sat on a blanket next to Harry and herded some cats. In the center of the gazebo, within a cozy feeding trough, lay four-week-old Maisie Streich alongside her mommy. Fire Chief Mike Orize played Joseph. Dressed as Mother Mary in blue robes, Assistant Sheriff

154

Megan Elyse Streich, still on maternity leave after delivering Maisie, knelt by the manger. As the people of the town sang to the tune of the angels in the bandstand, the heavens erupted.

In the sky, a whistling came. Like the twinkling, lights exploded in the dark night above. Tails of light streaked across the sky.

Declan, in his turban of sheets, came up to Harry and grabbed his shepherd's staff, shaking it. "Do you see what I see?" shouted Declan.

"Wow!" said Harry. "It's the cloned drones. They're back! That means the curse must have been lifted!" Harry said. Harry picked up Harvest and ran to his parents, who stood at the Clock Tower. "I'll be back," he said as he handed Harvest into his dad's arms. Harry ran across the green as the Christmas music rose into the sky. Harry looked and saw a figure cutting through the lamplight of Magic Row and shouted.

"Samson! Samson! Is that you?" Harry called as he ran toward the figure standing in front of the magic shop. With each breath, his heavy heart grew lighter.

In the wintry haze of the cold air, Harry did not notice the crown setting on top of the magician's head still tilted askew.

"The very one," called out the figure. "Whew. What was *that* all about," Samson said softly.

Harry ran across the snow-dusted square.

"Samson! I was so worried I would never see you again! But how? How did you get free?" Harry asked.

"Why, by you, of course, Harry," Samson said as he held out both arms to receive Harry. "I have always said you have the magic to do impossible things. Rabbit is a good tutor. And let me say, there was no iota of Halloween in it."

Harry reached out and hugged his teacher.

"I am just so glad you are back!"

Samson hugged Harry. "Merry Christmas, my friend."

"Merry Christmas, Samson."

"And of course I will come."

"Come to what?"

"Christmas dinner. Didn't your mother want you to invite me, I mean that is, if I got back from Austria's Black Forest in time?"

157

Harry looked up at his teacher. "Yes, but of course. But how did you know?"

"I don't care much for eating, but I do rather enjoy your family. And while you are at it, you might want to invite Thor. His folks don't celebrate Christmas. And he has already asked for my help." Samson looked pensive a moment. "Well, I steered him in the right direction. He wants me to help him with his animals. And I can do that easily enough, thanks to you."

Samson opened his hand, and it was on fire. He smiled at Harry and closed his fist, extinguishing the flame. The magician gave Harry a gentle wink.

"You really are back, aren't you?" Harry said. Harry noticed a great light upon Samson's face as he smiled at his student. The light seemed to be a reflection from above. Harry looked toward the sky.

158

The hundred drones had formed one great Christmas star twinkling at the very center of the night. On this one truly magical Christmas Eve night, the good people of Sleepy Hollow were finding their way lit by the light that shone brightly in the darkness.

Encore

GOD BLESS US, EVERYONE!

At the Moon family Christmas dinner, there were two guests—Thor Treeodin and Samson Dupree. Thor was sitting down for the first Christmas dinner of his life. Imagine that. The hound, Half Moon, lay underneath the table, gnawing out the bliss from his new Christmas bone. Who knew there could be such ecstasy from an old bone? And after the Christmas blessing, not knowing the protocol, as if they were Christmas crackers, Thor quietly handed small gifts to each family member and Samson too. Thor even gave one to tiny Harvest. Harvest beamed at the attention.

160

"Now, don't put the bag in your mouth, Harvest," said Honey. "Presents are to open, not eat."

"Don't say don't to me," said Harvest, waving the present over his little head.

"Why, what is this?" said John Moon as he pulled a ring made of brass out of Thor's present to him. He weighed it in his palm and encircled it 'round his index finger.

"You tell him, Harry," Thor said, awkwardly.

He butted his proud chin in the air as if

entreating Harry, *over to you.* Thor was still a guy of few words.

Harry knew what the ring was. It was the heavy brass ring that Thor wore when he wanted to punch somebody. Harry knew Thor carried it in his pocket just in case he wanted to defend himself. But Harry had looked beyond the ring, beyond Thor's tough-guy jacket, and the lightning bolt of the Viking god emblazoned on his leather lapel. Harry had gazed upon Thor's heart.

161

"Thor's giving you his fight ring, Dad," Harry said. "I'm sure you understand. It's kinda a big deal. Between us guys, you get it?" Harry said with an asking voice, not absolutely sure. Thor nodded his approval.

John Moon's eyes glistened with tears. "I do understand, Harry. And Thor, I understand in a way far deeper than you may ever know. Thank you, my young friend. You are very much loved and appreciated in the Moon home."

"Merry Christmas, Mr. Moon," Thor said.

When Harry looked over at his new friend, he felt a bursting of his own heart. Just days earlier, Harry had wanted vengeance as he faced down the darkness that enshrouded the Sleepy Hollow Magic Shoppe. Rabbit had encouraged him to look for a miracle instead. He had found more than one this Christmas.

"Now, let's eat!" said John Moon in a gleeful tone.

The entire Moon family helped with the preparation for the meal. On the table, family style, was a luscious roast turkey with all the trimmings. On the finest china were abundant heaps of savory vegetables. Honey lifted the stone lid from a soup tureen. It seethed with heat, making the alcove dim with its delicious steam.

Samson was not much of an eater. Most Guardians were not. They feasted on the feats of goodness born from selfless hearts. But it would be rude if he did not join the family wolfing down the turkey and chestnut stuffing, made with so much love and care.

163

Harry watched as his teacher lifted the Christmas turkey to his mouth and ate.

"Wow, you actually chew and everything," said Harry.

"Stick with me, kid. I am full of surprises," replied Samson.

"I plan to," Harry said, smiling.

From his aged and weather-scarred face, as

timeless as the figurehead of an old ship might be, Samson returned the smile of his capable, deserving student.

For the umpteenth time, Harry saw the light of a thousand stars twinkle in Samson's eyes.

His teacher had returned to him.

And that was the most amazing Christmas miracle of all.

All it took was giving a guy in a bomber jacket a chance to show off the deep love of the Great Magician with a petting zoo.

With a great clatter, Samson rose from his chair. The entire family turned to see what was the matter. Harvest was choking on the ring John Moon had received from Thor. Samson opened his power palm over Harvest's mouth, and the ring fell into his palm.

"Thank you, Harvest," said Samson as he flipped the brass ring back to John Moon. And then, Harry watched as a tiny bunny hopped from Harvest's mouth by the same continued pull Samson had made with his power hand to retrieve the ring.

Instead of crying, Harvest went quiet. The bunny with a pink nose and lop ears wrapped his paws around the child.

"You are just full of surprises," said Harry to Samson.

Samson shrugged. His quiet eyes were sparkling with Christmas happiness.

165

"I got a bunny just like Harry," Harvest shouted.

Harvest turned to the little bunny and said with great confidence, "Now, don't say don't to me."

"I wouldn't count on that," said the bunny.

Harvest hugged the bunny anyway.

Harvest looked from his booster chair at

the people around the table. The child had the most wondrous eyes as they turned toward each person around the table and glistened. And why shouldn't those eyes hold wonder? For as Charles Dickens had said so many years ago in *A Christmas Carol*, it was good to be a child "and never better than at Christmastime, when it's mighty Founder was a child himself."

As the feast was cleared from the table, Harry pulled his iPad from the credenza. He propped it up on the table so that all could see the lyrics to "Joy to the World" on the screen.

Around a dessert spread of mince-pie, red-hot chestnuts, cherry-cheeked, baked apples, and an immense twelfth-cake, the Moon family stood with their two guests. They sang the lyrics from the carol displayed on Harry Moon's iPad.

This was Harry's carol. He wrote it himself.

For life is what we make of it at
*   Christmastime.*
Each of us brings to it their own

special rhyme.
Through our hand, we can all bring a glow,
This we know. The Great Magician tells
  us so.

We have the song to make Christmastime.
Let the winter air ring with our special chime,
For there will always be trouble in this land,
So there's always a chance to lend a
  helping hand.

After the long and happy holiday where town hall was closed from Christmas Eve to the first of the year, Margaret Toledo and the other town clerks returned to their windows. It was always strange coming back after such a long hiatus, but the clerks were refreshed and ready. There was a certain joy in returning to the day-to-day life of the office give and take. The clerks lifted up their counter screens to the lines of people needing help with every kind of permit and license.

Mayor Kligore's office at the end of the first floor was decidedly raucous this first morning

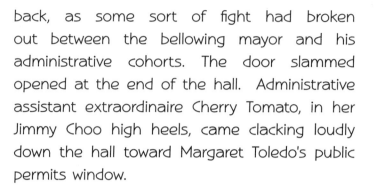

back, as some sort of fight had broken out between the bellowing mayor and his administrative cohorts. The door slammed opened at the end of the hall. Administrative assistant extraordinaire Cherry Tomato, in her Jimmy Choo high heels, came clacking loudly down the hall toward Margaret Toledo's public permits window.

"YOU!" Cherry Tomato shouted, her mouth grim and irritable. Pointing an accusing finger at black-haired Margaret, Cherry then turned and aimed her finger at the open door of Mayor Kligore's office. "NOW!" She shouted.

Flustered, Margaret placed her tidy paperwork into a folder and marched out of the clerk bay. She followed the clack-clack-clack of Cherry's Jimmy Choos. As she stepped closer to the door of the mayor's office, Margaret could feel the coldness of the mayor's heart. She walked into the outer office and discovered all sorts of critters-gone-wrong sitting in cold darkness. There was Ug, Oink, and Lady Dra Dra in a spider-black wig. They looked past her with hollow eyes as if she wasn't even there.

"Just the clerk I wanted to see," barked Mayor Maximus Kligore. "Since when do we give permits for the gathering of animals, Mrs. Toledo?"

"Since 1684 when Elias Dunwright held the first cow and goat auction in the green," said Margaret plainly and without agitation.

"And when, *re-cent-ly*, have we granted such rights?"

"You know very well when," Margaret Toledo said. "It was Christmas Eve of this past year. No doubt, it is why you look at me with such fury. But long before you, Mayor, for nearly four hundred years, Sleepy Hollow had been an agrarian community, sustained by fields and animal husbandry. We have granted permits to the Treeodin Family for years for their animal parade. Our history is full of people here who love and respect animals. Everything was tidy and neat during Treeodin's event. They left the premises as they had found them. There were no reports of vandalism or misconduct."

"Only yours, Mrs. Toledo," said the mayor. "What took place was an abomination. At your parade—" said Mayor Kligore.

"It was not my parade. It was the Treeodin's parade," replied Margaret.

"This was clear vengeance on the part of the Toledo family to get back at me for berating the barber husband when he intentionally sliced up my neck in his establishment!"

"Are you really that distant that you cannot see, Mayor? Your screaming at my husband is between you and him. I am Clerk of Public Permits. I have a responsibility to the people of this town, and if they want to celebrate their animals, they have every right to do so under section 512b of the public gathering permissions, which has been in force since 1684, three years after the establishment of this fair township." Margaret took a deep breath and let it out slowly as Cherry Tomato looked on with scowling eyes. "And if angels or demons or whatever under heaven wish to partake in such proceedings, that is not my affair nor yours.

But I do believe, as the Christmas carol goes, where there is nature, Heaven shall sing. And who are we to stop any angels who just happen to be in the neighborhood?"

"GET OUT OF MY OFFICE!" Kligore screamed.

"Merry Christmas, Mayor, and may every day be merry for you in this new year!"

"GET OUT!" Kligore shouted again. At that moment, it seemed Mayor Maximus Kligore was the only one in Sleepy Hollow that believed that he was fighting a winning battle against the light of holidays, which are rooted in the long traditions of men, women, and children.

So, may it be for you, and may it be for all of us, that the magic of the Great Magician finds its way into our lives each and every day.

171

MARK ANDREW POE

Harry Moon author Mark Andrew Poe never thought about being a children's writer growing up. His dream was to love and care for animals, specifically his friends in the rabbit community.

173

Along the way, Mark became successful in all sorts of interesting careers. He entered the print and publishing world as a young man, and his company did really, really well.

Mark became a popular and nationally sought-after health care advocate for the care and well-being of rabbits.

Years ago, Mark came up with the idea of a story about a young man with a special connection to a world of magic, all revealed through a remarkable rabbit friend. Mark worked on his idea for several years before building a collaborative creative team to help bring his idea to life. And Harry Moon was born.

In 2014, Mark began a multi-book print series project intended to launch *The Adventures of Harry Moon* into the youth marketplace as a hero defined by a love for a magic where love and 'DO NO EVIL' live. Today, Mark continues to work on the many stories of Harry Moon. He lives in suburban Chicago with his wife and his twenty-five rabbits.

BE SURE TO READ THE CONTINUING AND
AMAZING ADVENTURES OF HARRY MOON

Harry Moon's
DNA

Helps his fellow schoolmates
Makes friends with those who had once been his enemies
Respects nature
Honors his body
Does not categorize people too quickly
Seeks wisdom from adults
Guides the young
Controls his passions
Is curious
Understands that life will have trouble and accepts it
And, of course, loves his mom!

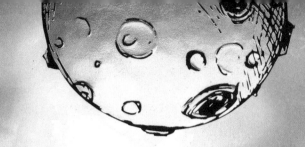

Coming Soon!
More Magical Adventures

POSTER INSIDE!

HARRY MOON

FIRST LIGHT

MARK ANDREW POE

FOR MORE BOOKS & RESOURCES GO TO
HARRYMOON.COM

POSTER INSIDE!

HARRY MOON

TICKLISH

MARK ANDREW POE

Honey Moon's
DNA

Builds friendships that matter
Goes where she is needed
Helps fellow classmates
Speaks her mind
Honors her body
Does not categorize others
Loves to have a blast
Seeks wisdom from adults
Desires to be brave
Sparkles away
And, of course, loves her mom

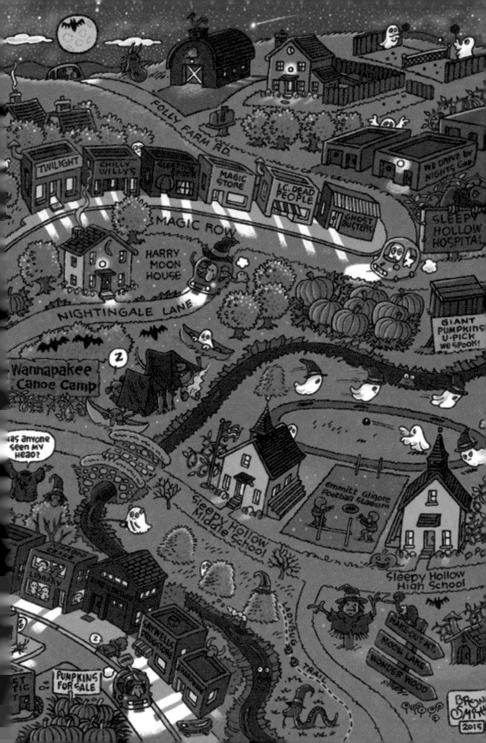